Yvonne Neville was born in Rangoon, Burma, where her father had rice mills. She spent most of her working life in medical research and lectured in Gerontology. During an eight-year gap, she and her husband Robin ran a country inn which they bought when he was made redundant. A life-long lover of classical music she also enjoys craftwork, designing, writing and drawing, gives talks on a variety of subjects and has six great grandchildren to keep her on her toes.

Yvonne Neville

PIECES OF EIGHT

AUSTIN MACAULEY PUBLISHERS™
LONDON • CAMBRIDGE • NEW YORK • SHARJAH

A CIP catalogue record for this title is available from the British Library.

ISBN 9781398456693 (Paperback)
ISBN 9781398456709 (ePub e-book)

www.austinmacauley.com

First Published 2022
Austin Macauley Publishers Ltd®
1 Canada Square
Canary Wharf
London
E14 5AA

Thanks to one special proofreader who remains nameless, but she knows who she is.

Introduction

Eight women travelling together to compete in the International Eisteddfod at Llangollen are trapped between landslides on a Welsh country road and forced to spend two nights in a Spartan youth hostel. As they get to know each other better, secrets from their pasts are revealed one-by-one each one more shocking than they could have ever imagined.

Set sometime in the nineteen-fifties.

"Is everyone belted-up?" called Marion over her shoulder as her seven passengers settled into their minibus seats. "No singing, and not too much talking, save your voices for tomorrow," she added.

"Yes boss," replied Rene thinking to herself, *Bossy bitch, treats us like kids from her school.* To be fair, they should save their voices on their way to Llangollen to sing at the Eisteddfod. Being a small group, only six men and eight women, every voice counted. Leader Marion added her fine mezzo-soprano voice to the blend, when not on the piano or conducting. They usually sang a cappella while only using the piano for rehearsals. On stage, they relied on pitch pipes or Marion's trusty old tuning fork. OK, thought Rene, she is the boss, we better behave.

"Wagons roll! Next stop coffee," Marion said brightly as she pulled away from the kerb disturbing the large puddle the vehicle had been standing in. She hoped she sounded more confident than she was feeling. Although a competent driver, she already found the unfamiliar controls of the hired minibus slow and heavy to respond, not at all like her own Mini Cooper sports car. They had all been looking forward to the trip, not just taking part in the Eisteddfod but the whole adventure. It had been Marion's idea, the eight women group together, and she had volunteered to drive. The men were all making their own way in cars, some taking wives and families to make a bit of a holiday of it. What they hadn't foreseen and couldn't control was the weather. After a long dry spell, the rains came like a monsoon. For three days and nights, it rained relentlessly and it didn't look like letting up any time soon.

As Marion's spacious front drive was big enough for several cars parked while they were away, it had been the obvious starting point but they got soaked loading in their cases and locking up. Shrugging out of wet coats as they settled, the inside of the bus was already steaming up. Marion turned the heating on. The windscreen wipers were barely coping with the torrential rain. This would be a long, difficult drive, not the happy jaunt Marion had anticipated. She shivered in the damp atmosphere or was it nerves?

The very early start meant that the roads were mercifully quiet, allowing Marion to swerve round the huge puddles which sometimes stretched more than halfway across the roadway. Many suburban roads were flooded but once on the motorway, there was less standing water. However, the constant spray thrown up by the rush hour traffic was hazardous and wearying. Despite this, they made steady progress and arrived safely at their first planned stop. Marion had suggested that they save time by bringing sandwiches and flasks for a picnic. Sadly, in the downpour, there was no option but a quick dash under an umbrella or with a coat over the head, to the service station toilets, and a climb back on board the bus. As soon as the cups were drained and the food wrappers gathered up, it was a subdued party that was ready to hit the road again. There was no point in lingering. They were in open rolling countryside. They just couldn't see it through the sheets of rain.

Marion drove doggedly on. Her eyes were smarting, and a headache was pulsing in time with the push-pull of the windscreen wipers. In the gloom, everyone was driving with headlights full on, and the glare from oncoming traffic was dazzling.

By late afternoon, the motorways were left behind, and they were on narrow country roads. They should have been in Llangollen by now, but the waterlogged roads had slowed the journey. The women were chatting quietly and anticipating the proper meal they had promised themselves as soon as they reached their hotel.

* * * * *

Such a varied band they were! The youngest was just forty and the oldest over sixty, the rest somewhere in-between. Their only connection was music. They knew very little about each other's backgrounds as they rarely mixed socially. Little did they know that was about to change.

MARION, a teacher, head of mathematics at a prestigious school, is married to a member of parliament. She is handsome, tallish, and well-proportioned. She is always well-dressed, usually in a dark suit with a silk scarf to soften the neckline and add a touch of colour. She is blessed with light chestnut wavy hair, elegantly cut very short. She has music in her soul and revels in her role as leader of the Kelvin Singers, the group that she founded not quite ten years ago.

GLORIA is a popular GP in her uncle's five doctor practice. She's good with children and stern with their parents. Smokers can expect to face a fixed glare, pursed lips, and a frown as she enumerates the many harmful effects of cigarettes. Gloria is the "daughter of the Manse". Her name derives from her mother's admiration for the silent movie star Gloria Swanson. Her father never got that connection, he just thought it had a nice religious ring to it. Fair to say she does not quite suit her glamorous name, being lean and bony, spinsterish, and outspoken. She dresses rather primly in tweed skirts with box pleats, knitted twinsets, and sensible shoes. She wears no make-up. Her brown hair is neatly curled... kept that way by the overnight wearing of curlers. She possesses a deep, warm alto voice. She is unmarried.

RENE is also unmarried. She is ex-army, was an officer, and is now an administrator in the Scottish National Trust. She is tall and striking in appearance, always immaculate in sharply pressed trousers, a crisp shirt, and one of many beautifully embroidered jackets she brought home from postings abroad. Her fair hair, almost white blonde, is cut in a straight bob. She has a fine alto voice and as her recently pursued hobby is cordon bleu cooking, supper parties at her flat are a delight.

VERA is tiny and seems frail. One of the older members, she still retains a good soprano register. She rarely looks you in the eye and keeps her head down as if apologising for her existence. Her colourless hair is carefully styled but dull, and her features are always lined with worry. She wears expensive clothes, not shown to advantage by her demeanour. Extremely good shoes, handbags, and jewellery suggest she is not lacking in money, although she never had a career. She is widowed and lives with her only son.

PHIL, christened Philomena, a name she hates, is an enigma to her fellow choristers. She has a first-class honours arts degree and speaks several languages but seems devoid of ambition. She is devoted to the chapel where she is the housekeeper cum secretary to Father Bernard. She is an excellent reader of music and has the voice of an angel. Her other interest is Scottish country dancing. She has displayed, occasionally, a gift for traditional Irish dancing. She is a squat shape with a short neck and thick ankles. She wears baggy clothes in neutral colours and looks to all the world like someone's cleaning lady. Her plain face is topped by dark home-perm frizzy hair. She too is unmarried.

EVELYN's steel-grey hair is severely drawn into a tight bun. She is small, very thin and also wears nondescript clothes, but hers are neat and well-fitted. She seems determined to fade into the background. However, when she sings, she is transformed and can move an audience to tears with the rich tones of her mezzo-soprano voice. She is the manager of a private old people's nursing home and is devoted to the patients. Outside of the home, the Kelvin Singers and her church are her only activities.

HELEN is grossly overweight, and yet, she is a highly regarded personal assistant to a high-powered business tycoon. She tends to dress in flowery silks and wears either sandals or boots depending on the time of year. No one can remember ever seeing her in shoes. Her hair is always untidy, and her appearance is the antithesis of a successful career woman. She is divorced, childless, and shares a modest semi-detached house with her widowed mother. Despite her bulk, she has a high-range soprano voice.

KATHERINE, another soprano, is widowed. She is a history teacher nearing retirement who is athletic, enjoys golf, tennis, and hill-walking. Her bouffant curls were once blonde but are now snowy white. She is always smiling. She is of medium height and build, likes casual, sporty wear, but always looks good. She has a ready, sometimes wicked sense of humour, is great company, and gets on really well with everyone. She sings with a rich warm tone.

A mixed group indeed, the only link being music, the enjoyment of the weekly choir practice; carol concert at Christmas to entertain old people in Residential care, and an annual concert to raise funds for charities as varied as themselves. For the female members of the Kelvin Singers, the next four days would change them forever.

* * * * *

They were driving through what felt like a dank green tunnel of dripping trees and shiny bushes. The clouds were down to eyebrow level. Glowing faintly in the distance was a flashing light. A policeman in yellow oilskins waved them to a halt with his torch. Marion hadn't realised how hard she was gripping the steering wheel until she had to prize her fingers off. She saw, to her surprise, that her perfectly manicured hands were shaking. Not like her at all.

"Where are you heading?"

"Llangollen."

"Sorry, there's a landslide up ahead. The road is closed."

"Can we turn and find another way?"

"Unlikely. There's another landslide behind you now. It's going to be tomorrow before any attempt to clear the blockages can start. You're stuck for the night, I'm afraid, but there's a Youth Hostel a little way on. With all this wet weather, they have no one staying at the moment. They should be able to take you in for the night. Follow me."

He climbed back into the police car, and Marion tailed him several hundred yards up the hill ahead until they pulled off the road in front of an imposing Victorian villa with a porticoed entrance. Rene joined Marion and followed the policeman into the building, leaving the others meantime stretching cramped limbs and eyeing the grey edifice through the still pelting rain.

Inside a gloomy hall, a big old-fashioned brass bell was screwed to the reception desk. The policeman punched it. At once, a glass window behind the counter slid open, and a lugubrious face looked out.

"The roads are blocked in both directions. These people need shelter for the night."

Marion said, "There are just eight of us if you have room."

"I daresay we have room. Rules are on the notice board. We don't do dinners. Just breakfasts."

At this point, Rene strode forward, "We will need a meal. We've had nothing since this morning. You must have some food."

"I'll get the wife." The face disappeared, and a thin woman in an overall came through a door and said, "I'm Mrs. Jackson. My husband and I are the wardens. We don't keep many stores."

"Are there shops nearby?"

"No."

"Well, let me see what you do have," said Rene, "and we'll see what we can rustle up."

When the police car drove off, cases were hauled out of the minibus, and everyone got thoroughly wet again. Mr. Jackson led them up the stairs to the two dormitories, one for males, one for females. In each were four two-tier metal bunk beds. A washroom with four sinks and two toilet cubicles went off the female dorm. Later inspection found the male accommodation had four sinks, one long urinal, and one toilet cubicle. "Spartan," commented Helen, who liked her creature comforts.

"Where is the bed linen?"

"We don't do bed linen," said Mr. Jackson. "You bring your own sleeping bags."

"Well, we're sorry Mr. Jackson, but we have a hotel booked in Llangollen that comes with bed linen, so we do not have sleeping bags to hand," said Helen.

"There's blankets and pillows in them cupboards then," he said and hastily retreated downstairs.

They began pulling blankets from the shelves. Some of the cupboards were locked. Helen wandered through from the washroom, shaking her wet hands.

"There are no towels," she said. "Oh look," she pointed to a notice pinned to the wall TOWELS MAY BE HIRED BY THE NIGHT.

"That's alright then," Helen said in a sarcastic tone with a loud sniff.

"It's cold up here. Let's leave this just now. We can sort it all out later," said Gloria. Downstairs again, they were greeted with the news that the telephone lines were down but that there would soon be a hot meal. That meant that they had time to take in their surroundings. The entry hall would have been spacious if it weren't for the long coat stands with many hooks and the long racks for footwear. A notice on the wall read NO BOOTS BEYOND THIS POINT. To one side, was a large room with long wooden trestle tables where Rene and Evelyn were putting out cutlery and plates. The tables were unpolished but well-scrubbed so it could have been worse. The room on the opposite side was of a similar size. Both rooms had large oriel windows overlooking the road and the parking area where the minibus sat. This must once have been the front garden.

A huge marble mantlepiece dominated one wall and housed a wood-burning stove which was giving off a welcome heat and pleasant aroma. Round the fireplace were three large squashy sofas. Two card tables with light wooden chairs were against the wall opposite the fireplace. In the oriel window space were two easy chairs flanking a spindly what-not table bearing a hammered brass pot which contained an enormous fuchsia plant covered with pink and purple ballerina blossoms. It was incongruously luxurious in its drab setting. The waist-high wooden panelling was scratched and worn, and the paper on the wall above the dado was faded and cracked in places. There was very little left of the once-grand ambience of the villa, aside from the ornate cornice and central rose of the ceiling, all in need of some paint.

Rene appeared from the kitchen at the back. As a military person, she was well used to taking charge of what had to be done. A large apron covered her immaculate shirt and trousers, and she was bearing plates of food. There was a stampede into the room with the tables.

"We are having tomorrow's breakfast now," she announced.

"Tomorrow's breakfast will just be porridge or cornflakes."

What Rene had found were twelve sausages, twelve bacon rashers, twelve tomatoes, and a tray of eggs. This she reckoned would suffice for the hungry eight. With loaves in the freezer, there were slices of toast, and there was tea and instant coffee. It was a feast, and she held back just enough milk for breakfast in the morning. Now that the meal was over, Rene organised a clearing and washing team while others settled around the fire. Marion added some fresh logs, and they savoured the wood smoke smell. When they were all together again, Marion said, "I'm really sorry I didn't get us to Llangollen. I don't even know where we are exactly."

"You don't need to be sorry. It's not your fault."

"I wonder if the men were ahead of us. Maybe they made it."

"We'll find out tomorrow. That's if there is a tomorrow!"

"Look at the rain. Is it ever going to stop?'

The rain was still pelting down, and despite being a "summer" evening in July, it was almost as dark as night. Marion still felt a sense of guilt but she was pleased with the way her fellow travellers had accepted this unfortunate situation.

* * * * *

Gloria, sitting in one of the comfortable chairs at the window, pondered her problem; her dilemma was not knowing what to do about it. Feeling the need for guidance, she decided to take the plunge and seek the advice of her friends. She cleared her throat and somewhat dramatically made her announcement.

"I have a confession to make." Everyone turned towards her.

"I have a son," she said.

It was no exaggeration to say that a shock wave travelled around the room. There was silence until Gloria continued, "I want you to help me decide what to do."

Everyone was stunned. It was unthinkable that strait-laced Gloria, the product of a devoutly religious upbringing should have a son nobody knew about.

"I think," said Katherine gently, "You'd better tell us all about him."

"He's twenty years old, and his name is David." Gloria paused before beginning to explain. She had met his father, also named David, at university, both studying medicine.

"We very quickly became inseparable. My mother arranged for digs for me with another girl, and it was fine, but when she quit in the second year, David simply moved in instead. Father never knew that I wasn't still sharing with Fiona." She grinned ruefully, "We had so much in common as well as medicine, music, and art. We both worked hard. We seemed to spur each other on in our studies, but we snatched time for concerts and galleries, operas, and films. Somehow, we never talked about the future beyond graduation. In the summer, when I was at home, he went off to learn to fly. He told me his father had a title, and there were estates in England and Australia as well as Scotland, but as the youngest son, David wouldn't be inheriting anything. Instead, he set his heart on joining the Flying Doctor Service in Australia. Only at our graduation did I find out that his father was a Marquis and that David already had his ticket for Australia. He left almost immediately." Gloria paused. No-one spoke. She put more logs on the fire. They spluttered and sparked in the silence,

"I guess you know what happened next."

"You found out that you were pregnant?"

"It was a bit of a shock because we took precautions." "Maybe we got careless."

"Did you tell him?"

"No." Again, Gloria paused and took a long breath.

"All I ever wanted was to be a doctor," she went on.

"Father's brother had a place for me in his practice whenever I qualified. That's what I wanted. I didn't want a family, and I didn't want to go to Australia."

Gloria's voice faltered, less confident now, wondering what they were thinking, but she continued.

"I know my father would have disowned me. He was very strict, and it would have broken his heart."

"So, what did you do?"

"My mother was sympathetic, and she came up with a plan. She had some money of her own she insisted I borrow. We told Father and Uncle John that I had a short-term appointment in a Mother and Baby Home to get further experience in obstetrics and child-care. This actually was true. The home was in Southern England, Exeter, and I worked there until I was booked in as a patient. The baby was born and adopted the next day. I had to give him a name; his adoptive parents didn't change it. I returned home and joined the practice. I had no regrets. I still have no regrets."

"So, what's the problem?"

"I received a letter from the Adoption Society. My son is seeking contact. I don't know what to do. Should I meet him?"

"Of course, you should," said Katherine, "imagine not knowing who you really are!" Katherine, who could trace her ancestors back to the Norman Conquest, was horrified.

"You must tell him who his father is too," said Helen. "It's his right to know he belongs to an important family."

"Maybe, but I don't feel I want to. Everything was fine until that letter came."

"Come on, Gloria. Think of it from his point of view. Look we're all a little shocked, but we know you are a kind and decent person. Of course, you'll do the right thing for him, won't you?"

* * * * *

The question hung in the air. Gloria remained silent, but Rene suddenly stood up, walked to the window, and turned around to face the room. When she spoke, there was a chilly bleakness in her voice.

"I know what it's like to have no family, no family history. I would give anything to know where I came from."

She sat down abruptly; her face contorted with emotion.

"I was found in a cardboard box on the doorstep of an orphanage. I lived there for sixteen years and no one ever came to claim me. I can't begin to tell you how important origins and background are when all you have is a vague hope that somewhere there is someone who would like to find you again. Please, Gloria, meet him and tell him." The others nodded, but Gloria rose without a word, left the room and headed up the staircase.

"I need a drink," said Helen. "I've got a bottle in my case." She followed Gloria. Both came back down shortly, each carrying a bottle. Helen had whisky, and Gloria brought brandy.

"We all need a drink," said Rene. She disappeared into the kitchen and returned with eight glasses on a tray with a jug of water and a couple of small bottles of Coca-Cola and lemonade.

"Don't worry," she said "I've left IOUs for these. It can go on our bill. There are a couple more crates of these in the store."

As the drinks were poured, Katherine produced a block of vanilla fudge from her handbag which she divided neatly into eight pieces. Suddenly the glass reception window slid open, and Mr. Jackson said, "No alcohol in Youth Hostels."

"Thank you, Mr. Jackson, for your timely reminder, but we aren't youth hostellers, and this is medicinal," said Gloria.

"I'll drink to that. Cheers!" Said Phil.

A short time later, Mr. Jackson brought another bucket of logs and took away the empty one. He kept his eyes down; he didn't want to see the raised glasses in his domain.

"Thank you, Mr. Jackson," called Gloria as he scuttled back through the kitchen door.

"I think Rene, if you are willing to tell us, we would like to hear your story," said Katherine. "Start at the beginning." Rene nodded. As soon as she started to talk about the orphanage, Rene almost had to stop. It came so vividly to mind; she could hear the footsteps echoing in the long corridors and smell the mixture of dust, carbolic soap, and beeswax. Only when visitors were expected were the tins of beeswax brought out to polish everything: furniture, banisters, doors and, the staircase but only the risers, not the treads that would have been too slippery. Most of the time, the lustre was achieved the hard way, with considerable effort. Floors, whether wood or tiles, were scrubbed with carbolic soap and a hard bristle brush. This was most often performed, kneeling, as a punishment. Hands nipped, nails went soft, eyes and nose stung in the steam until the water grew cold, and then the hands turned blue.

Rene was told she was abandoned, just a few days old, on the doorstep of Rosebank and immediately placed in their care. There were no clues to her identity other than the newspaper lining the box, The Scotsman, predominantly an Edinburgh paper.

She was given the name Irene but prefers Rene. Until she was old enough to go to senior school, she knew no other place. The juniors were taught by teachers who came daily. They came promptly at nine and left equally promptly at one. Rene had the distinct impression that the teachers didn't much like Rosebank. Where it got its name was a mystery as not a single rose, or any other flower for that matter, ever bloomed around the gloomy building, black from many years of sooty atmosphere. Neighbouring buildings had been sandblasted back to pale sandstone beauty but not Rosebank. The level "playing" area was entirely covered in sharp gravel resulting in trips to see Matron if you fell and had grazed knees, elbows, or hands.

Then, young patients were obliged to try not to cry out as she gleefully picked out larger pieces of grit with tweezers and then scrubbed the rest of the dirt from the wound with a stiff nailbrush. The nippiest disinfectant was then liberally applied before a square of pink lint, followed by a square of green waterproof material, were secured by a stiff white bandage. Every child in Matron's care knew that the rest of the world could rely on comfortable, stretchy Elastoplast dressings for skinned knees, but Matron's outdated ways persisted.

"Were you tortured?" interrupted Vera in a small voice.

"Not torture. Just the way things were done. Punishment was tough but meted out for our own good, we were told."

Minor misdemeanours by the little ones were dealt with instantly, Matron taking a hairbrush from her apron pocket. Over her knee, down with the knickers and the little bare bottom was spanked hard. Rene remembered that it could be sore for hours, making it hard to sit still in class.

Anything deemed a sin or crime meant being sent to the Guardian's office for his brand of punishment. It didn't matter what age you were, you had to bend over the arm of a wooden chair; pants were then unceremoniously pulled to your ankles, and he took a leather belt, known in Scotland as a tawse, and laid it on with enthusiasm. Each hit created bruising on your front or ribcage from the chair and a nasty weal on your bottom. A further indignity, while still bent over, was feeling his podgy fingers being pushed inside you. Rene would say nothing, determined not to show that it hurt, assuming it was part of the punishment. She did, however, try not to merit a visit to the Guardian.

Later, Rene became aware that Matron didn't send girls to the Guardian when they were menstruating, no matter how bad their behaviour had been. All the girls hated their "periods." They were messy. Each girl was issued two sanitary towels, one for the day and one for the night. While one was worn, the other was hand-washed and dried on the radiator. Well aware that there was such a thing as a sanitary belt, they could only wish for such refinement as the loops on their pads had to be safety pinned to their underwear. It was nasty and degrading. The dorm always seemed to smell; of old blood and the bleach that was poured liberally down the toilet pans. It was possible, when you went to senior school, to skip school dinner and save some money from the allowance doled out daily. Rene's first "big spend" was a packet of Tampax, having read about the disposable tampons from a magazine smuggled in some pinched from Doctor or Dentist waiting rooms. It was a great feeling grown-up and cocking a snook at the stingy institution she had to call "Home."

* * * * *

Some of Rene's friends had family members who sometimes sent gifts, but these were frowned upon and either returned or shared. Providing luxuries was actively discouraged. In her entire life at Rosebank, Rene never received or wore one piece of new clothing. Small wonder when she left school to join the army, she was thrilled to have brand new sets of uniform and all the gear that went with it. She ruefully admitted that there was nothing strange about khaki underwear. Pants and bras at Rosebank tended to end up that colour after multiple washings with clothes of all colours.

"Rosebank wasn't all bad," said Rene, "but I was bullied by a boy called Iain Mackie." Even as she said the name, she felt the anger rise as she explained how the bullying started. She had gone outside for a bit of air and was horrified to see a big, strong boy sitting on the low wall that separated the playing area from the three-foot-wide no-mans-land beyond which were the seven-foot-high, spiked metal railings. Over his knee was a little girl, wet knickers at her feet, whose little red bottom he was slapping as hard as he could.

"How dare you," shouted Rene.

"Aw, ah dare," he said, "dae ye want some yourself?"

He pushed the little girl roughly off his knee. She landed with a real thump on the sharp gravel. He made a grab for Rene, but she was too fast. She elbowed him in the face, catching him off balance so that he toppled backward into the long grass, nettles, and dandelions. Rene picked up the wee lass and fled indoors.

"From that day, he stalked me at every turn," said Rene.

"He would grab me from behind and try to throttle me, but I was pretty good at fighting back. If he was with his little gang of thugs, I had less chance of escaping. I would be brought to the ground and kicked savagely. I suspect, on more than one occasion, I had a cracked rib or two."

"Did you report him?"

"No. I didn't want to give him the satisfaction."

"That's awful."

"One time," Rene continued, "my bed was covered with soil and all mussed up. I got a thrashing for being dirty and untidy. I'm sure Iain Mackie was responsible, but I had no idea how he could have got into the girls' side of the building unseen. I wondered if he bullied some other girl into doing it for him. He tried to get me at school, but that was more difficult. There were always teachers and monitors about. Anyway, he was a year older than I, so all I had to do was wait until he left. My last year wasn't too bad, and then I joined the Army."

They had all seen photographs of Rene in full officer's dress uniform red jacket with brass buttons and lots of gold braids, and a floor-length dark blue skirt. She looked magnificent, smiling for the camera like the cat who got the cream.

"Why did you leave the Army?" asked Helen, who had long fancied herself in a Wren's uniform. That was before she had somehow spread in all directions to her present unforgivable size, a good depth of lung capacity for singing being the only benefit.

"Oh, lack of opportunity. I rose through the ranks quite quickly but seemed to have reached as far as a female is allowed to go"—Rene paused for what seemed a long time and then went on—"actually that's not the real reason. As this seems to be confession time, I might as well tell you that I was cashiered, dishonourably discharged."

Every eye was on Rene, every mouth open. Only the battering of rain on the window broke the silence.

"There you have it, my shameful secret."

"What on earth did you do to get cashiered?" asked Katherine.

"I assaulted a junior officer, "Rene replied.

"Why?"

"When I was posted to Berlin, I was warned that the RSM, Regimental Sergeant Major, was a sadist; his punishments were nasty and brutal."

For a moment Rene, shut her eyes and shivered.

"My first encounter with him was a shock. It was Iain Mackie."

There was a chorus of drawn breaths, and Rene continued.

"At first, he didn't recognise me, but I was aware he was looking intently at me as if he felt he should know me."

Rene bent her head as she relived the eventual moment of recognition.

"Well, well, Ma'am. I see we have mutual friends and a common background. We must see if we can get together to reminisce."

The cold steel in his voice belied his "friendly" greeting. Of course, he could do little to upset a senior officer directly but he could make a misery of the lives of men and women under her command and this he did. He was subtle and cunning and sometimes she could have wept for the demoralised catering staff. Rene pulled herself back to the present and continued.

"One night after the inter-battalion rugby match which we had won, a trio of MP's brought Iain Mackie into the empty mess where I was checking cutlery and crockery supplies.

He was very, very drunk. I got them to lay him on a bench in the gymnasium and promised I would sober him up with hot coffee. Instead, I fed him coffee laced with sleeping pills."

As Rene paused, there was a merry smile hovering on her lips.

"I have to explain before I tell you what I did, that Iain Mackie had grown an enormous moustache of which he was inordinately proud. The ends were waxed and curled. In its way it was magnificent. When I was sure he was virtually unconscious, I fetched scissors and a razor and I shaved off one side only. Then I left him where he was."

Rene giggled and one by one the others joined in.

"What happened then?"

"He was apparently incandescent with rage. Nobody knew how he got there or who did it. I knew that the MPs who brought him in were from a different battalion. He made such a fuss that the CO was obliged to take action. It was announced that if no-one owned up, everyone would have various freedoms and privileges withdrawn. I couldn't let that happen so I confessed."

"Being thrown out of your whole career seems a bit harsh," commented Helen.

"But you see, as a senior officer my behaviour was grossly inappropriate. I had to pay the price. It was worth it, "she added.

"What a shame!": said Marion, thinking of Rene's career not the moustache.

"How come with a dishonourable discharge, you got a job with the Scottish National Trust a pretty august body?" asked Helen, ever the practical one.

"I told the CO about the orphanage and he wrote me an excellent reference said I was a first-class officer subjected to severe provocation. Besides, there was a retired Brigadier on the Trust's interview board. The CO had a word with him. That's my story."

"You should have got a medal, not the boot!".

* * * * *

Having learned new sides to Gloria and Rene, everyone was in reflective mood. Marion was thinking that Vera looked very poorly. She had noted that Vera ate very little of her share of the fry-up. Maybe not a good traveller or something else troubling her. Marion planned to keep an eye on her unaware that Gloria, too, had decided that Vera didn't look well and needed watching. As the logs settled in the stove with a little volley of sparks, thoughts were turning to bed or bunks.

"How about singing something nice and peaceful to untangle our nerves before we head upstairs?" said Katherine. "How about Ave Verum?"

Marion hummed a note and led seamlessly into them quietly singing Mozart's Ave Verum Corpus, the Latin words slipping from their lips. Only those facing it were aware that the reception window had opened. When the last gentle note faded away, Mrs Jackson was applauding.

"That's the most beautiful thing I have ever heard," she said.

"Thank you," said Marion.

"Is that what you are singing at the Eisteddfod?"

"No. It's just a piece of music we all love. We have Scottish songs for the competition. "Scots Wha Hae" which is a marching song and a Robert Burns love song "O Were My Luv Yon Lilac Fair.""

"I'd love to hear them too."

"We need the men for "Scots Wha Hae" but we'll sing the other one for you tomorrow before we leave, but right now we're ready for bed.

Mrs Jackson said "I'm sorry we don't have better beds for you. There's plenty of hot water from the Aga for the wash basins and the showers are electric. Here's the key for the towel cupboard."

"Thank you. We appreciate that."

"And so, to bed," said Marion, leading the way out of the room which was already cooling rapidly. Outside, the rain continued to fall in sheets.

Amid much hilarity, the shower rooms were located and the cupboards raided for pillows, blankets and towels. Looking at an exceedingly thin towel, Katherine commented

"My grandmother would have said that you could spit peas through it!" She handed them round.

"I don't need a towel," said Rene, "I've got one with me."

The pillows were lumpy and covered in a coarse blue and white striped ticking, matching the meagre mattresses on the bunks.

"First World War issue I suspect," said Katherine as she handed round the dank grey prickly wool blankets.

"There aren't any pillowcases. I don't suppose you have your own pillowcase, Rene?"

"As a matter of fact, I do," responded Rene. "I always travel with a pillowcase, towel, torch, kitchen knife and screwdriver. It's my emergency kit. Like the Scouts, I like to be prepared."

"Are we going to use the men's dorm too, so we can all have a lower bunk?"

"Oh no," said Vera. "Can't we all stay together?"

"Well, I don't mind being up top," said Gloria. "We shouldn't use the men's dorm in case more people get stranded and come here."

"That could be exciting."

"Ladies please," said Marion. "let's just try to get some sleep."

"Yes Boss. Get her swanning around in a floor length nightdress and matching negligee! Try climbing into a top bunk in that."

Marion, however, did just that. Helen was ensconced below, her bulk overflowing both the bunk and her winceyette pyjamas. With a bit of to-ing and fro-ing, all were finally settled and the lights put out with a brief round of "Good Night."

Balanced precariously, or so she felt, Marion was far from sleep. It was not entirely dark. A safety light somewhere outside gave a faint glow through the uncurtained window. Twice during the night there were furtive visits to the toilets and once a muffled expletive as a bare toe met an immobile object. Were they trying not to waken the others or unwilling to admit to the bladder affliction which is the lot of so many women approaching a certain age? Marion wondered if anyone was actually asleep considering the level of noise Helen was making. Her stentorian snoring reverberated to the rafters great grunt on the breath in and a whistle on the way out rhythmic as the tide, in out, in and out. Each snort sent a vibration up through the hollow metal frame of the bunks so there was nothing soporific for Marion with Helen below. Why, pondered Marion, did some people snore when others didn't. Probably Helen's obesity, the slack folds of skin around her jaw made her snore so loud.

Marion switched her thoughts to Vera. She was attempting to climb into a top bunk, holding on awkwardly and struggling when Phil said "You take the lower one, I'll hop up top." Vera's clearly not right. I'll speak to her tomorrow, thought Marion as she finally drifted off into a troubled sleep.

* * * * *

Breakfast was a subdued affair. Porridge, cornflakes, tea and coffee. Although there was bread in the freezer, there was nothing to spread on it and nobody fancied dry toast. There was no point in venturing outside as the rain had not let-up. The screech of tyres on gravel and the bang of car doors sent

31

everyone to the window. The policeman they met yesterday hurried in along with a fellow policeman.

"I'm afraid that the weather forecast is bad. There are thunderstorms on the way."

"Are the roads going to be cleared soon?"

"Not a chance."

"That means that we are stuck here. We've no more food," said Rene.

"Sorry, yes, there's no way you can leave for now but we have some stuff for you from the farm up the road. He said you'd be needing it."

Several bags and boxes were carried in from the police car. Rene's eyes lit up at the sight of trays of eggs, milk, butter, cheese and a big sack of potatoes and some turnips.

"Hallelujah! At least we won't starve."

After accepting grateful thanks for their help and promising to keep in touch, the two policemen drove away. A further round of coffees was proposed. It looked like the wardens had decided to throw their lot with the women as Mrs Jackson led Rene off to see what her small larder would yield for the common good. Mr. Jackson suddenly appeared.

"It's just been on the television. The Eisteddfod has had to be cancelled. The main tent collapsed under the weight of the rainwater. Two people were killed and others were crushed. They are in hospital."

"Oh my God! We don't know if our men got to Llangollen."

"Well, here's hoping, like us, they never got there."

"Amen to that."

Marion was siting opposite Phil and wondering why she didn't try to make more effort with her appearance. Even with her lumpy shape she could dress less frumpily.

"Phil, we know that you come originally from Ireland, but we don't know much about you. How about telling us more about yourself?'

"My parents came from Ireland but I was born and brought-up in Paisley. I've loads of cousins and aunties and uncles in and around Dublin. I spend four weeks with them every summer. Dublin's a great city, it's great fun and I love it. There you see, I'm not as staid as you think I am."

"I never thought you were staid," countered Katherine "just a bit serious. Besides you can't do country dancing and be staid. Remember I have seen you dancing."

"You devote a lot of time to the Chapel. What is it you do there?" asked Helen.

"Father Bernard was keen to have his predecessor's papers edited and catalogued. Father Connor was quite a literary figure. It was interesting work. I was happy to do it. Then I took over all of the paperwork."

"It does seem a waste. Your kind of over qualified for that aren't you?'

"You sound just like my parents. They are both academics and were very ambitious for me. I'm a big disappointment to them but that's their problem."

Phil couldn't help recalling the shouting matches. Her father's big red face even redder than usual, slamming his fist on the desk and saying how hard they had worked to lift themselves out of the bogs of Ireland. Her mother, tearfully saying she didn't understand why she spent holidays with the Dublin relatives when she could go anywhere in the world and meet clever and interesting people. Phil didn't recollect her parents ever going back to Ireland unless there was a funeral or a wedding and more often than not, they would find excuses not to attend.

"They kept nagging me. That's why I left home and moved into Father Bernard's home. It made sense to me and was cheaper than a flat of my own. I've got two rooms to myself which is all I need."

"But I heard you were also his housekeeper."

"If I had a flat of my own, I'd be housekeeping anyway. What's the difference?"

"I suppose if you put it that way. You can't still be cataloguing. You've been at it for years. Are there records and accounts to do?"

"You are a puzzle," said Katherine, "such a lowly job for such a well-read person. I think I agree with your parents."

There was silence. Katherine was sorry she had made that comment as if it was any of her business what Phil chose to do. She was about to apologise when Phil spread her hands wide and said "Since this is becoming such a soul-bearing get together, I might as well confess that Father Bernard and I have been lovers for more than ten years."

"Phil, you astonish me," exclaimed Gloria "You've never given the slightest hint."

"How many Hails Mary's does that require?" asked Helen and everyone laughed and then were embarrassed and went quiet again.

"You may as well know this too. We used the rhythm method of contraception but we didn't always get it right. We have two children, a boy and a girl. They live in Ireland."

"How on earth did you manage that without anyone knowing?"

"It was easy loose, baggy clothing and a month in Dublin on holiday. I have a cousin whose wife can't have babies. They're overjoyed to register the babies as their own. I see them every year but I'm just another auntie."

"Your doctor must have known," interjected Gloria.

"No," said Phil, "I never saw the doctor. I didn't need any medical treatment. I was absolutely fine both times. In fact, someone asked if I'd already had my holiday because I was looking so well."

Gloria could barely believe she could go through not one but two pregnancies without seeing a doctor although she could well imagine Phil positively blooming with health as many pregnant women did.

"Isn't what you're doing an awful sin in your faith?"

"Yes, it is but we don't feel like that. We call it nfinity and it's wonderful." Phil's eyes lit up, sparkling.

"It all began when Bernard had shoulder problems and a lot of pain. I offered to massage his neck and shoulders. One thing led to another and well you know we didn't mean it to happen."

Phil remembered the point when their relationship changed. They had been sitting side-by-side at the big desk trying to decipher the crabbed handwriting of a manuscript. Dating from wartime when the paper was scarce and of poor quality it was proving difficult to read. Paper was often used again and again. Rubbing out what was previously written made the surface soft and new writing fuzzy. Bernard stretched back and flexed his shoulders. He complained his neck was sore. She stood up and started to massage his neck

35

as she had often done for her father when he spent too long pouring over a book. Without thinking she pulled his collar to loosen the neckline and gently kneaded his shoulders.

She felt him relaxing and almost purring like a cat. When she stopped, he took her hand and kissed it? For a long time, they looked at each other slightly startled. Then he said "I want to kiss you." He pulled her onto his knee and they began a long gentle kiss. That's all it was, a kiss, but somewhere deep a fire had been lit.

It was a slow awakening for both of them. All was normal by day when they carried out their duties and tasks imbued with an inner glow of delight. In the evenings they held each other, exploring wordlessly. Strange and unreal this lasted several weeks and then the inevitable happened when he led her into his bedroom and shut the door.

"You know what I want to do," he said.

"Yes."

"Is that what you want too?"

"Yes."

As they were both virgins, it was a bit inept but nature and passion took over. She couldn't believe the sensation of completeness she felt. She remembered giggling and commenting that they seemed to fit perfectly together. Afterwards they slept like babies still entwined.

As time went by their secret love never waned. The days were spent in exquisite anticipation of the nights to come. Phil only had to think of Bernard to enjoy a clench in her loins. When Phil achieved orgasms, which was most of the time, it was ecstasy. Then there was the guilt. Both of them were all too aware of the enormity of their sin but they weren't going to stop.

"Does no-one suspect?"

"I don't thinks so. At all times we maintain the formalities expected of us but when the door is shut and the curtains closed, life is wonderful. We couldn't be happier. I know, when the time comes, we'll have to answer to God but not yet. How can anything so good be bad? How could anything so right be wrong?"

Heads were shaking all around. This was such a shocking revelation and coming from such an unlikely source, it was hard to believe but no-one could fail to see Phil's inner happiness.

"What's the rhythm method?" asked Evelyn.

"It's working out the regularity of your period and then timing things to avoid sex on the ovulation days between periods when you're fertile," answered Gloria.

Katherine said "I used to be a Marriage Guidance Counsellor and we often had young Roman Catholic couples referred to us for contraceptive advice. One young man came along on his own because his wife was at home coping with a toddler and a new baby. I asked him if his wife's periods were regular and he said "I don't know. We've been married for two years and she hasn't had one yet." There was laughter at that and the mood was lightened.

* * * * *

"Right folks, get the tables set. Lunch is coming," announced Rene. It's minestrone soup thanks to Mrs Jackson's pantry and the farm up the road."

Rene had put together stock cubes, tins of chopped tomatoes, a tin of mixed vegetables along with a bag of frozen peas, an onion, turnip, tomato juice and a handful of rice. There were rolls from the freezer, heated in the Aga, and butter.

"It's a bit short on onion, and no garlic, but we do have a wee carton of grated parmesan cheese to lend some authenticity."

Marion was sitting with the others finishing an after-lunch coffee.

"How are we off for tea and coffee?" She asked. The idea of running out of coffee was unthinkable.

"Plenty unless we were here for weeks," replied Rene.

They all jumped with alarm as a flash of blinding lightning filled the room followed almost immediately by a great crump of thunder.

"That was close. It was getting so dark outside I thought the storm wouldn't be long coming."

Marion was thinking how strange that half of them rushed to the window to watch the lightning flashes that were piercing the skies one after another, while the other half huddled fearfully together as far from the window as possible. The flashing display was spectacular and there was a strange smell in the air, like the aftermath of fireworks on bonfire night. The thunder rolled round the hills above the house and then the lights which they had to put on when it got so dark, went out.

"Oh, no! The power lines must have been hit."

"That's all we need."

Marion thought of the big torch she always had in her car and then remembered it was the minibus parked outside, not her car.

It was, of course, still daylight, albeit pretty dismal and darker now inside than outside. Mr Jackson appeared with a Calor gas lamp and a box of matches.

"You'll need this when it gets dark. The wife's looking out some candles too."

The thunder grew distant and the lightning less frequent. The storm had lasted more than an hour. The watchers returned to the comfort of the sofas round the wood burner. The atmosphere was humid, clammy and cheerless. The warmth of the burning logs was welcome.

Mrs Jackson carried in a box of white candles and some old-fashioned white enamel candle-holders with handles Wee Willie Winkie style.

"Please be careful," she said "we're not supposed to use candles."

"We'll be careful, Mrs Jackson, thanks."

Just as she turned away there was a sudden very loud noise like an express train in a tunnel and a series of ear-splitting bangs and thuds. A scrunching, scraping sound assaulted the ears and they rushed to the window to see what was happening. To their astonishment, they witnessed a fully-grow tree crossing the road, apparently under its own steam and accompanied by a number of smaller saplings and bushes. A wall of mud, stones and boulders then swept down the side of the house and across the road. Some of it swelled out round the front and swamped the car park They could only watch open-mouthed as the minibus began to move, slowly at first, but then it was simply swept sideways across the road. When its furthest wheels dipped off the road surface, it simply flipped over on its side. The wheels, now up in the air, spun on for a while and then stopped.

In terror, Vera screamed "We're going to be swept away!"

"No, we won't."

Mrs Jackson nodded. "We are quite safe. We often have some floods like this but the house is solid enough. We'll be OK. Don't worry."

"God knows how long we're going to be stuck here," said Rene.

* * * * *

Marion's feelings of guilt for proposing this venture were multiplying by the minute. Did she have enough insurance for the minibus? Were the men of the Kelvin Singers caught in the tent and maybe injured or worse, killed? Were they stranded somewhere like us, and how were they all going to get home?

"I'm so sorry I got you into this mess," she said.

"Don't be daft. It's not your fault."

"All the same, I'm frightened."

"This isn't like you Marion," said Katherine. "you're Mrs Supercool."

"Oh, I'm not. I make terrible mistakes."

"Nonsense, we've never known you to lose your sangfroid."

"Oh, I do, I did. I've sinned even worse than you, Phil."

Marion suddenly sobbed and covered her face with her hands.

"Marion, if you want us to believe that, you are going to have to tell us what you did that you think was so awful."

Marion shuddered, suddenly looking drawn and old, older than her years. She clasped her hands, closed her eyes and said "I had sex with one of my pupils."

The storm was completely forgotten. Everyone was in shock. Disbelief was evident on every face but further revelation was abandoned by the arrival of the same two policemen. They had been obliged to leave their car some distance down the road and wade through the mud and rocks surrounding the building.

"Is everybody alright?" one asked. Everyone nodded.

"We can see what happened to your minibus."

"What's happening now? We're OK but we have no electricity."

"Work has begun in the valley to clear the roads but there's a lot of flooding. Up ahead is still blocked and now we can't reach the farm."

"By the way," said the other policeman, "have you noticed the rain has stopped?"

Indeed, not only had the rain finally stopped, there was the merest hint of a watery sun.

"Thank goodness for that."

"Hallelujah," said Rene.

As soon as the police set off through the morass to reach their car, Rene went upstairs and fetched her torch which she laid at the foot of the stairs so that visits to the toilets would be safer. There were nods of approval and thanks but the silence remained unbroken until Helen spoke.

"Marion, you had better explain yourself."

Marion remembered, with great clarity, the day that Jack Miller appeared at the back of her 5th year class. Their eyes met and he gave her a little bow. Even then she felt a frisson of interest. He was extremely good-looking and he knew it. The girls in the class were already atwitter. Unlike the other boys who were all in school uniform, he was casually dressed but his chinos were well pressed. His shirt, open at the neck, revealed smooth tanned skin. A couple of days later, clad in school blazer, grey trousers, shirt and tie, he was even more handsome and devastatingly self-assured. By then she had learned from the headmaster that Jack was American. His father was a big-wig in electronics and travelled a lot. They had recently lived in Germany for a few years but they were now to be based in Scotland for a period. There was no mother and Jack happily went to school, often one of the international schools, wherever they were living.

Over the weeks that followed, she observed that he usually hung-out with the other boys, paying little heed to the gaggle of girls, never far away from him. She also noted that his school work, especially maths, was excellent.

One hot, hot day, Marion returned home from school taking pleasure in the cool of the big stone house that had been her husband Malcolm's family home. She loved its spacious rooms, traditional pieces of furniture, polished and well-loved for many years and mixed happily, she felt, with pieces she had added herself. She was greeted, as always by Paddy a big lumbering Golden Retriever, who waited patiently for her to let him out the back door into the garden. She very quickly peeled off her tights, sought sandals from the cupboard under the stairs and taking Paddy's lead she followed him out on to the lawn. They left by the gate at the side of the house for his customary short walk.

When they returned, she kicked off her sandals and lay down, eyes shut, beside Paddy savouring the cool grass beneath them. She was roused by a low growl from Paddy. A voice above her said "Hello Mrs Gibb". She was amazed to see Jack Miller offering a hand to Paddy who promptly licked it and wagged his tail.

"How did you find out where I live?" She demanded still shaken by his sudden appearance in her garden.

"I followed you from school."

She didn't know what to say to that. It was quite a short distance from the school and with the traffic a slow crawl it would not have been difficult to keep sight of her distinctive yellow car. She knew later, that he had tailed her on his bicycle. He sat down, uninvited, and she was disturbed by his closeness. He was tickling Paddy's ears. Paddy, of course, proceeded to roll on his back with delight to have his tummy tickled.

"Some watch-dog he is!" She commented not knowing what else to say.

"I have a way with dogs," he said and added, "and other animals." I bet you have thought Marion. She was acutely conscious of an electricity between them and somehow it was no surprise when he leaned over and kissed her expertly. She could hardly breathe and was only distantly aware that her panties had been deftly removed. The sex was quick, it was aggressive, it was wonderful. He stood up, straightened his clothes and said "You're a good-looking woman."

He looked at his watch and said "I have to go." He patted Paddy on the head and left by the side gate.

She lay still, confused, sated, tearful, terrified, ecstatic, disgusted all the emotions at the same time. Paddy came over and licked her forehead. What had she done? A scandal would ruin Malcolm's career in Parliament and put an end to her own, much-loved career. The garden was totally secluded with trees all around and the neighbours houses too far way to overlook it. How could she face Jack in the morning in class?

Recounting briefly that first occasion, she blushed with chagrin.

"I'm astonished," said Gloria.

"I'm ashamed," said Marion.

"What happened next day at school?"

"Nothing. It was as if it hadn't happened."

"So, it was only once?"

"No, it wasn't only once. He came on Mondays and Thursdays. Five o'clock on the dot and he left at five thirty. He came on his bike, parked it in the front garden and carried his school bag. The neighbours got to recognise him. He was very polite. On Thursdays he often arrived just as our cleaning lady was leaving. I had maths book laid out on Malcolm's desk in the study at the top of the stairs. She would tell him to go up to the study and she would let me know he had arrived. I told Malcolm I was providing extra tutoring for the boy to help him get a university place."

"Are you still doing it?"

"No."

"How long did this go on for?" asked Helen.

"Nearly two years."

"My God."

During the summer holidays, Malcolm and Marion always spent two weeks with her parents along with Paddy and then left Paddy with them while they had two weeks somewhere in the sun. Jack spent the summer sailing with his father in the Mediterranean and at other breaks they went skiing or climbing.

"He didn't come if I told him not to, when Malcolm would be home. We always used the spare bedroom which was just across the landing from the study."

"Weren't you afraid of getting pregnant?"

"No. I knew that couldn't happen. We have no children because I had an ectopic pregnancy that left me so badly damaged that I was sterilised."

Marion and Malcolm had discussed, at great length, the possibility of adopting but he was embarking on a career in politics which would be demanding and she made it clear she didn't want to have to live in London plus she valued her teaching post. Malcolm's elder brother James and his wife Freda had three children and a fourth on the way, Fiona, Finlay and Forbes usually nicknamed Fee, Fi, Fo. No doubt the new one would be Fum. As fond aunt and uncle they saw the children quite frequently.

"What ended it?" asked Evelyn.

"He went back to America with his dad."

That was another day blazoned in her memory. Jack had been with her as usual on the Monday. On Tuesday the Headmaster casually remarked "It's a pity we're losing young Miller. He's been an excellent student and he's done well. They are returning to the States."

Marion stumbled back to her classroom. She asked Jack to stay behind at the end of the class.

"When were you going to tell me, you were leaving?"

"I don't do tearful goodbyes."

"When are you going?"

"Tomorrow. I've a letter for you from my father. Don't worry I haven't told anyone. Thanks for everything Mrs Gibb." He shook her hand and was gone.

"What was in the letter?"

"An effusive thank you for all my extra help getting him through his exams so well. I felt like a fraud."

"Have you heard from him since?'

"Not a word. It's five years since he went. I don't understand how I could take such risks. I love Malcolm. To be honest I feel used and dirty. I think I was just a convenience for Jack."

"Do you think he had other women on other days?"

"I wouldn't be at all surprised."

"Wow! I don't know how you could let it go on so long."

"I couldn't help myself besides I was afraid if I tried to stop, he would have threatened to tell someone. I was terrified."

"Strikes me you were the victim of predatory youth," said Rene.

* * * * *

It was obvious that the little gleam of sunshine had been just that a little gleam. It was now dull and dreary again albeit blessedly dry. Rene announced that despite no electricity, teas and coffees were available. The hot water jack and the big tea urn both being electric, a big old kettle had been hastily rescued from a back cupboard and it had been on the Aga since the power failed. It had come to the boil at last.

"God Bless the Aga, it's oil fired and there's plenty of oil in the tank," said Rene.

Katherine was going through games in the cabinet on the end wall calling out "Cribbage, Dominoes, Backgammon, Drafts, Chess, Halma, Ludo, Tiddlywinks, Snakes and Ladders and there's umpteen decks of cards."

"Who plays Bridge?" asked Rene. Only two responded to that.

"Can someone show me how to play Cribbage?" asked Helen.

"Sure, I will, "said Katherine. The pair took over one of the card tables and were soon engrossed.

"What's Halma?" asked Evelyn.

"It's a bit like Drafts, not as clever as Chess, but it can be played by two or four players. I'll show you if you like," offered Phil and soon those two had hunted out a checkerboard and emptied out the set of little "men".

Meanwhile Gloria was nursing a cup of coffee and watching Vera closely. She was very pale and sitting very still. She hadn't even reacted to the horror of Marion's confession. When she realised that two big fat tears were rolling down Vera's cheeks she hastened over and put her arms around her.

"It's alright Vera. We will get home eventually."

Vera continued to sob. The others gathered round.

"What's the matter Vera?'

Gloria hugged her more tightly but Vera winced and tried to stifle a cry of pain. She immediately unclasped her.

"What is it?"

"My elbow hurts."

"Gently Gloria began to examine Vera's arm.

"Let me get this jacket off." This clearly caused Vera a lot of pain and it was easy to see why. Her whole arm was a livid black and blue. Gloria feeling around the elbow was alerted to the crunch of bones.

"My Dear, I am pretty sure there is a nasty break in there. When did that happen? What did you do?"

"I fell," replied Vera.

"When?"

"Last week."

"Why didn't you tell us?" Vera didn't reply.

Gloria went on to say "I don't think that's quite the whole truth. What are these? Who did that to you?"

She was pointing to little, angry red marks all over her forearm. She pulled the jacket from Vera's other arm. Holding it up, it too was scared.

"These look very much like cigarette burns. Vera, who did this to you? You must tell us."

Vera stifled another sob and said "My son."

"I really did fall."

"You mean he pushed you, "said Rene.

Vera's face crumpled but she said nothing.

"That's what I thought," said Gloria, nodding to herself.

As they all tried to comfort her, she broke down completely and cried piteously. They were all aghast.

"I'm going to make that arm more comfortable and get you some painkillers," said Gloria.

"There's a first aid box in the hallway. I'll go and get it," said Evelyn. The box yielded the usual cotton square which all good Girl Guides (and Boy Scouts) knew could be folded into a temporary sling and a bottle of Disprin tablets. Once Vera's arm was immobilised and she had swallowed some pills, Marion whispered, "now just tell us what's been going on. Remember we are all your friends and maybe we can help."

"It's not his fault," said Vera through her tears, "the business isn't going well and he gets home angry. It's been failing ever since my husband died and young John took over. They used to row all the time because John didn't think they needed to spend money on new equipment and young John did."

"What kind of business?"

"Stationery. We make notebooks and envelopes and cardboard stuff like that but the demand is going down and the materials, especially paper, are getting dearer."

"Just because he's angry, why does he taken it out on you?"

"There's no-one else."

"Vera, that's no excuse."

"I know but…"

How could they understand, thought Vera. They don't know he's just like his father. They don't know he's behaving just the same way his father did only he didn't leave scars on his wife.

Vera's life had always been tightly controlled by a domineering man. When she was young her father vetted all her friends and because none found favour, her social life was very restricted. Piano lessons and singing in the Church Choir were the only leisure activities permitted. He didn't approve of girls showing themselves off on tennis courts and certainly not in swimming or on bicycles. She was not allowed to attend further education (dangerous in women, he said) or a career. The females in his life did not require to work as he was an adequate provider, he decreed. Her mouse-like mother was neither comforter or friend, too frightened herself to stand up for her daughter.

When he deemed her old enough, her father selected a suitable husband from among his own acquaintances...... a man only slightly younger than himself. Vera accepted her fiancé gladly assuming it was an escape but he turned out to be just as overbearing. He already had a house, furnished with antiques and she was not allowed to make any changes at all. He chose her clothes, escorting her to the very best shops four times a year when he selected dresses, suits and coats from the seasonal garments that met his approval. She rarely even got to try them on as she was, and remained, a standard size. She always knew she should be grateful. The clothes were classics, beautifully made from superior materials and she felt good in them but would have liked to make her own choices.

He allowed her to continue the music lessons and the choir. She had to attend many functions with him but he frowned whenever she spoke or expressed an opinion. At first, if she offended him, she had her knuckles cruelly whacked when they got home. Later he was even more violent, often hitting her with his fist for her own good, he said. Sadly, she rarely knew what she had done or said wrong. Because of her upbringing it never crossed her mind to leave him. Where would she go? Her father would have been furious. She tried to tell him what was happening to her but he rounded on her shouting that he couldn't be doing with hysterical women.

"Go home and do your duty to your husband," he brusquely commanded. So, the beatings went on.

* * * * *

When it came to her wifely "duty" sex, she didn't get any choices there either. When he wanted it, that's when it happened although he didn't seem to derive any pleasure or enjoy it very much. For her, it was painful and degrading and worrying was she doing something wrong again? But mercifully swift.

The beatings stopped abruptly when she was pregnant. He was unusually solicitous, making sure she attended the surgery and the ante-natal clinic. It was a happy time. He was thrilled to be expecting his son. He told her this many times and paid no heed to her reminding him it could be a daughter.

"Nonsense," he said, "I want a son. I need a son for the business." Vera often wondered what would have happened if she had produced a girl. At least the sex stopped once he had Young John.

After the birth, the beatings began again, usually because Young John was a fretful baby and a snivelling child and she couldn't keep him quiet. She never achieved any kind of rapport with her son. He seemed indifferent towards her. He was packed off to his father's old school but during the holidays when he was home, he was witness to his mother being abused. Indeed, it was obvious to Vera that he enjoyed the spectacle of his mother's pain and humiliation.

When Young John joined the business as he was expected to do, there were countless rows. Sometimes the large ledgers were brought home to study but Young John had not proved himself much of a mathematician. Economies were considered since profits were falling.

One evening when Vera was sitting quietly sewing, while the disputes went on, Young John pointed at her and said

"Well you don't have to spend so much money on clothes for her."

"Don't you dare say that," said John, "I am a man of means and my wife must be dressed accordingly."

Vera made the mistake of saying she didn't need new outfits every season as she had plenty of clothes in her wardrobe but they both rounded on her to shut-up.

It was one of those nights of endless bickering between father and son that John suddenly stiffened and fell forward clutching the edge of the desk. He had never had a day's illness in his entire life but at that moment, Vera became a widow.

Young John could hardly wait until the funeral was over to get his way in the business, to buy all the new equipment his father had resisted and to diversify and develop. However, he was in for a big shock when the will was read. Vera had inherited not only sole possession of the house but also half the firm. Her son was apoplectic. He had already planned to sell off the house and antiques to help the business finances but Vera was able to veto that ploy. She didn't much care what he did with the business. Young John wasn't clever or academic. Indeed, at school his marks were adequate at best but pretty woeful in most subjects so it was no surprise to Vera that his great ideas for expansion did not succeed. That's when the real torture began. The cigarettes burns were his specialty but he could be as violent as his father as well. She had to visit her dentist urgently when he knocked two teeth out.

One day he stormed into the house, slamming the door shut so hard it rattled the walking sticks and umbrellas in the hall-stand. Vera was playing the piano. He came straight to her and slammed down the lid of the keyboard narrowly missing the fingers she had fortunately snatched away. She retreated to the kitchen, picked up something to eat and sneaked up the back stairs to her room. For the first time ever, she locked her bedroom door. She could hear him battering round, banging things but she ignored the noise. Eventually it stopped. When she ventured down in the morning, the piano was in pieces. The hatchet that had been used was lying on top of the splintered wood and tangled strings. The piano stool was on its side and the sheet music kept inside it was scattered and trampled all about.

Vera set the stool upright again, gathered up all the music and replaced it in the stool which she moved to behind the big couch. The debris she left as it was.

The following day men arrived to remove the mess. Young John tried apologizing for the destruction of the piano even offering to buy her a new one but she didn't respond. All he wanted, he said, was sole control of the business and a half share in the house. He was convinced that was what his father intended and the lawyer had got it the wrong way round. He wheedled and pleaded and tortured her until eventually, she gave in. He already had the papers drawn up and she signed them.

When she finished her account of her plight, it was her friends who were apoplectic.

"Vera, that's awful. We never knew any of this."

"You've given it all away."

"Not quite," said Vera, showing a little spirit.

"I was perfectly happy for him to have all the business. It's failing anyway. I signed over my half quite happily but when I came to the house, I didn't use my proper signature, just a made-up-name in a squiggle. The silly boy didn't arrange for the signing to be witnessed so I can deny I ever agreed to sign half the house to him."

"Well done, girl," came the cry from Helen.

"We'll work out a way to collect evidence and get him convicted."

"Oh no," Vera cried, "I don't want him convicted."

"But you can't go on living with him," said Gloria. "We'll get you out of that house, somewhere safe. In fact, you can move in with me until things are sorted out. There's plenty of room in the old manse and you can play the piano as much as you like—it's hardly ever played."

"We'll go with you," said Rene, "and pick up all your lovely clothes in case he tries to damage them."

"What will you do when he finds out about the house?"

"I don't want the house, I don't even like it, but I'll need the money so I'll probably put it up for sale but give him time to look for somewhere else."

"He doesn't deserve that much consideration."

"No, he doesn't," said someone but Vera was smiling. Her friends were all round her and she felt the warmth of their affection like a sunbeam falling on her.

* * * * *

Rene started taking candles through to the tables and getting set up for their evening meal. She came quickly back to say "It's really quite cold in there now. I think we'll stay here and eat."

"How are you managing without electricity?' asked Helen.

"Fine," said Rene "the Aga's wonderful and God bless the Jacksons for their canny store. Apparently Mr Jackson liked his baked beans and Mrs Jackson purchased the tins in multiple packs."

"Tonight," said Rene with a flourish of the tea towel in her hand, "we are having baked potatoes with Heinz Beans and grated cheese. And there's dessert to follow. I've rescued a pack of twelve choc ices from the bottom of the freezer which is now thawing rapidly."

"Rene you are great. You've worked a miracle."

"I don't know about a miracle. It's hardly the loaves and fishes. I've earmarked the last loaf for tomorrow's breakfast along with the last of the butter but after that we will need a miracle or turn cannibal."

The Jacksons were invited to join them but she said her husband was too shy and they would just stay in their own "parlour". With the candles creating a festive ambience they consumed the food in good spirits rounding off with the unexpected treat of choc ices.

More cribbage was played and a game of drafts was started but when the dishwashers returned from the kitchen, it was Phil who was said "OK, who's next for the confessional?" Everyone laughed but no-one answered and then Katherine said "I have something to tell you."

No-one spoke but looked up expectantly.

"I'm getting married next month."

A chorus of questions followed that announcement.

"Who to?'

"When did this happen?"

"How did you meet him? Did you get swept off your feet?"

"Give the girl a chance right, tell all."

"I've known him for a very long time, in fact we went together when we were at school."

Katherine who was rarely without a smile was now beaming broadly and blushing as she recalled the accidental meeting just a few weeks previously.

Katherine was in the supermarket looking for a nice ripe melon to halve with her neighbour as both of them found a whole melon too much for themselves. A deep voice at her shoulder asked "Are you testing that melon for ripeness? How do you do that?'

"Yes, I am," she replied.

"Will you show me how?"

"You just press the end gently like that with your thumb. It should give a little. If it, doesn't it isn't ripe. If it's too spongy it's over-ripe."

"I see. Well thank you."

She turned to find a tall, broad-shouldered man with a mop of curly white hair and a wide grin in a tanned face. Chocolate brown eyes met her gaze and, in an instant of recognition, she whispered "Murray?"

He looked stunned for a moment and then responded "Katherine?"

Immediately she was swept into a bearhug, still clutching the melon.

"It's been long time," she muttered, her words muffled against his pullover.

"A lifetime. You look splendid as gorgeous as ever."

"You're not so bad yourself, but are you sure you don't need your eyes tested?" She protested, laughing. Indeed, she thought, he was as handsome as ever. She took in his checked shirt, open at the neck, under a fine woollen jersey, grey trousers and leather loafers.

"Have you finished your shopping so we can go and have a coffee somewhere? I want to know what you've been doing all these years."

"A couple more things, and I'd better buy this slightly squashed melon. There's a coffee shop here in the store, or there's a nice pub round the corner."

"Even better."

She was glad he'd settled for the pub because the coffee shop was often very noisy. She too wanted to find out what he had been doing. Later in the day, their coffee morphed into a pub lunch as the years melted away.

They met at secondary school and dated throughout their fourth and fifth years. They were members of the Friday Club and the Badminton Club, which met after classes. Every Saturday they went to the cinema together. Murray was quiet and thoughtful. She remembered how loyal he was to his father, even though he was very strict, not allowing him the same freedom many of his peers enjoyed. The only weekday evening out he had was for the Scouts. Every other evening, he had to concentrate on his school homework after delivering evening newspapers. Murray's mother died at his birth, and his father's elder unmarried sister moved in to take care of her brother and nephew. She was a cheerless, resentful woman who became more and more bitter and sharp as the years went by. His father had a newsagent shop and spent long hours there, so it was a cold home life with not a lot of love shown. During holidays, Murray helped in the shop.

This was in sharp contrast to Katherine's home life. Both her parents were teachers, and every summer, they spent nearly all of July and August on the Isle of Arran, off the west coast of Scotland. They rented the same cottage every year, located right on the shore. Only a grassy bank separated it from the sandy beach. It was approached by a narrow lane, with tufts of grass growing between rough tyre tracks. There, she and her brother ran barefoot all summer, in and out of the water.

Nearby were several other cottages all occupied by the same families who came, like them, every year. One interesting family who came for a month consisted of two doctors and their four children. They ran wild too, the only rule being they had to clean their teeth properly, but so long as they were in the sea often enough, they were exempt from washing.

The day before they went home, they all had their hair washed. It was such a happy-go-lucky time. Sometimes they went climbing or hiking or would take a boat out and go fishing. Fresh mackerel caught, gutted, and fried on the beach was a frequent treat. Of course, the memory can play tricks, but Katherine couldn't remember it ever raining.

All her memories of Arran were sunny. Yet she did recall one dramatic event when some of the adults went for an evening stroll cum climb and got caught in one of the sudden storms that engulf the mountains without warning. They were inappropriately dressed and had to be rescued. Katherine remembered one of the women in a gypsy blouse, navy shorts, and sandals shivering uncontrollably and ashen with fatigue and fright.

During the rest of the year, besides being included in many of their parents' pursuits, Katherine and her brother were encouraged to develop their own hobbies and activities. It was an open and loving household with few restrictions.

By the end of their fifth year, Murray made no secret of his intention to join the Royal Navy. Katherine was going into her sixth year before university. At the end-of-term ball, they danced together all evening. Murray walked her home and, despite a tearful farewell, they made no promises to keep in touch. With the resilience of youth, it was one door closing, another door opening. Katherine never heard from him again, but she always wondered what happened to him, her first love.

Now it was time to find out.

* * * * *

Murray got his question in first. "I guess from the ring on your finger that you're married?"

"I'm widowed. My husband, Bill, died four years ago,"

"Family?"

"Two daughters both grown-up with their own flats, so I live alone now. They are both high flyers with great careers and aren't showing any signs of settling down and starting families. They don't even seem to have time for boyfriends," she sighed.

"Do you live near here?"

"Yes, not far. The girls found my flat for me, and I'm very happy with it. Bill and I had a lovely home, but it was much too big for me on my own. How about you?"

"Well, you know I joined the Navy. I had a great life. Life at sea was everything I hoped for. I saw the world and made some great mates."

"I see you too wear a wedding ring?" she commented.

"Yes, but I am widowed as well. My lovely Laura died last year. I have two sons, both married, and there's a baby on the way. I'm looking forward to being a Grandad. We all live in New Zealand."

"So, you're just here on holiday?"

"Sort of. I was a bit restless and had a notion to visit Scotland. In all the years I was away, I returned only once for my father's funeral."

"I'm sorry to hear that your father died. What happened to your aunt?"

"After I left, she started going to the shop with Dad to help out. Apparently, she sort of thawed out. You remember what she was like?"

"Yes, I do."

"She got on really well with the customers, and when Dad died, she took over the shop. She's retired now, living in an Old People's Home. I've been to see her, but she doesn't know who I am. She doesn't seem to know who she is herself."

"I'm sorry. That's sad."

"So, where did you meet your wife?"

"She was a New Zealander. The ship was in port, Christchurch, and my pal Simon was going ashore to attend his brother's engagement party and took me along. Laura was there."

What a day that was! Simon's brother picked them up from the ship and drove them to a large barn building out of town. There were lots of guys already there with piles of crates of beer. It was already pretty rumbustious, and Murray thought it strange for an engagement party with only one female on the scene. He wondered if this was the bride-to-be.

She was a lovely-looking girl, slender, athletic limbs and dark hair.

Murray sat for a while watching all the back-slapping and trying to understand the banter, which with the broad accents could have been a foreign language. To his surprise, the girl came over and sat beside him.

"I don't know you," she said in the straight-talking New Zealand way.

"I'm just here with the bridegroom's brother Simon."

"Ah, from the ship?"

"Are you the bride-to-be?'

"Heavens no. She'll be here soon with all the girls. I'm here early because I'm helping with the catering. Has no one offered you a beer?'

"I promised to get Simon safely back to the ship, so I'd better stay sober. "

"Impossible," she said, "but if you really don't want to start drinking yet, you could help me set out the food. My name is Laura."

"I'm Murray, and I'm at your service," he said, saluting.

They set out the food, unwrapped dishes of salads and trays of sandwiches and pies.

"This is an awful lot of food," he commented.

"They need it to sober up so that they can start drinking all over again," she explained. Someone was frying sausages as the girls arrived in a flurry of flouncy frocks. After months of austerity at sea, it was dazzling. Somehow, he managed to stay close to Laura throughout the party. She didn't seem to be anyone else's partner. There was some dancing to music played on a record player and, although a poor dancer, Murray found himself enjoying the fun, especially when he had his arm round Laura.

As the party began to break up, he helped her clear up the leftovers, wash some dishes and leave the place tidy. They loaded empties into a van.

"Can I maybe walk you home?" he ventured.

She laughed. "I don't think so; it's fifty miles."

"Oh."

"Anyway, I'm staying here for a few days, camping with the others. If you don't have to be back on the ship yet, why don't you stay too? Everyone bunks down in the barn."

It was Simon, a couple of days later, who got the smitten Murray back on-board ship. Laura returned to her father's sheep farm, but they wrote to each other all the time. He actually proposed by letter, was accepted by letter, and when he had leave, they were married. He remained in the Royal Navy until he had served his time while she continued to work with her father and the sheep. They got together whenever they could.

Eventually, he left the Navy and became a slightly bemused sheep farmer. Their two sons now run the farm. They took over when Laura got ill, and Murray needed to look after her during a long battle with cancer. It was a heart-breaking time. She remained stoical and brave to the end but he was all too aware of what it cost her to hide the pain from all but him. He was quietly relieved when she finally succumbed. A sick sheep on their farm would not have been allowed to suffer so long.

"I'm sorry, Murray, that must have been awful," said Katherine.

"My Bill suffered a massive stroke just sitting in his chair. It came out of the blue, after a life free of illness. He was always proud of his fitness. He never regained consciousness and died two days later. I was devastated, but the girls and my friends and colleagues at school carried me through the worst bits."

"Colleagues at school?"

"Yes, I'm a history teacher. I had to keep going for the children in my classes. Some were just about to sit their most important exams. That helped me a lot."

"I bet it did! Fancy you, a history teacher!"

"Bill and I had a lovely life together. We used to go camping in France every year with the girls, but we got more adventurous when the girls were too old to want to come with us. We had wonderful trips to far-away places."

"We'll have to compare notes on far-away places," he said.

They talked for a while, and when they left the pub, she asked, "Where are you staying?"

"I'm in a B&B just along from the supermarket."

"With Mrs. Dickie?"

"That's right."

"She'll look after you well. I'll drive you there, and I'll point out my flat when we pass it on the way."

They walked back to the supermarket carpark for her car, and when they drove past her building, she said, "One up on the left. Would you like to come for dinner tonight?' She surprised herself because she hadn't intended to issue such an invitation just yet.

"I can't think of anything I'd like more," he said, smiling that broad smile that lit up his face.

"What time?"

"Make it seven."

"It's a date."

Once home, she did a quick tidy and put a bottle of rosé wine in the fridge and checked there was a bottle of red in the wine rack; because of her practice of cooking meals for two, eating half and freezing half, the meals she had prepared for tonight just needed to go in the oven. When she moved into the flat with its little kitchen, she didn't intend to squeeze in a freezer, but the girls had insisted, and right now, she was glad. She had oatcakes and cheese for afters and a bowl of fruit, and there was ice cream in the freezer. She filled the coffee percolator, ready to switch on when they sat down at the table which she had set, not too formal but with rather more attention to detail than her usual solo dining.

Murray explained that he planned to hire a car and visit all the places he remembered but felt daunted by the traffic and the narrow roads. Katherine quickly volunteered to drive him around.

"I'd like to visit them too. That's if you would like me to?"

"I'd like that very much."

"Come round tomorrow morning for coffee, and we can make plans."

"That's a date," he said "another date?" he added, laughing.

* * * * *

And so, they spent happy days together, both reminiscing and finding out about their separate lives. He was sad to see the cinema they used to go to had been converted into a block of flats, and the church he attended was now a private house. Both were shocked when they toured his old newspaper round to find how much that particular neighbourhood had deteriorated. The streets were littered with rubbish, and all the shops, including what had been his dad's, were empty, windows boarded up. Even their old school had moved to a new site, and the old buildings were demolished to make way for an up-market housing estate.

"No more railings to climb if you were late for Assembly," Murray commented.

Katherine laughed, remembering all too well the visit to the Rector's office when she'd been caught in the act. At 9 o'clock sharp, the bell rang, and all gates were locked except the main one, which just happened to be in full view of the school offices. Scaling the railings was a "criminal" offence warranting tedious punishment writing "lines."

The days turned to weeks, and their joy in finding each other again never flagged, so it came as no surprise when he asked if she would marry him. They were on a day trip to Arran, where she showed where they had holidayed all those years ago. He had already passed muster with the daughters who were truly happy for her, so she was thrilled to say, "Yes."

"Congratulations," they all said at once and crowded around to hug her.

"When's the happy day?"

"Two weeks on Tuesday. We've only just fixed the date. Murray has spoken to his family. He said his boys are looking forward to meeting me. He promised he would be home in time for the birth of his first grandchild, so we're flying out to

Singapore and then sailing to New Zealand. That will be our honeymoon."

"Lovely! But you are coming back?"

"Oh yes. We think maybe six months there and six months here will keep us in touch with everyone."

"That's a great idea."

Marion picked up Rene's torch and made her way up the stairs, but she was quickly back down with a bottle of champagne in each hand and the torch held precariously under her arm.

"I bought these in case we were celebrating a win at the Eisteddfod."

"Or drowning our sorrows," said Helen.

"But we really have something wonderful to celebrate," continued Marion. Glasses were produced, and corks popped. So, it wasn't chilled properly, and it was in a tumbler, but no one cared. The Jacksons were persuaded to share the fun.

Vera declined the fizz, asking if she could perhaps have cocoa instead.

"Very wise," said Gloria, "because I'm going to give you more Disprin."

"We don't have any cocoa," said Mr. Jackson, "but we have drinking chocolate. Will that do?"

"Oh yes, please," said Vera, who was soon sipping a mug of velvet-smooth hot chocolate unaware that Rene had decided to sacrifice the rest of the milk to make it. Tomorrow's breakfast, thought Rene, will be a masterclass in what can be achieved from a drastically reduced pantry.

Still full of bonhomie, they finished the evening fulfilling their promise to the Jacksons by singing Burns Love song.

O were my love yon Lilac fair,
Wi' purple blossoms to the Spring,
And I, a bird to shelter there,
When wearied on my little wing!
How I wad mourn when it was torn
By Autumn wild, and Winter rude!
But I wad sing on wanton wing,
When youthfu' May its bloom renew'd.
O gin my love were yon red rose,
That grows upon the castle wa';
And I myself a drap o' dew,
Into her bonie breast to fa'!
And there wi' tremblin' luv's unrest, I'd plead my passion
a' the nicht
Seal'd on her silk-saft faulds to rest,
Till fley'd awa by morning's licht."

"You would have won first prize with that," enthused Mr. Jackson, his saturnine features unusually wreathed in smiles.

Mrs. Jackson, visibly moved said, "What lovely people you are!"

Thinking back to the earlier revelations, no one was too sure about that. What they wondered could possibly still be to confess.

* * * * *

Breakfast was a subdued start to another day of their enforced stay.

Rene had worked her magic and they ate a kind of omelette but baked in trays in the trusty Aga. Mr. Jackson informed them that the oil tank was more than half full, but he was running out of logs for the wood-burning stove, which kept the damp atmosphere at bay. There were ten to feed, and there were ten slices of bread in the very last loaf, and there was just enough butter left to spread on them.

"Coffee drinkers," said Rene…… "will have to ballot for the last coffee. We still have tea, but there's no milk."

"This has to be good for the waistline," said Helen.

A fresh gloom descended on the party. The rain had begun again, just a drizzle, but it made the sky leaden. The view from the window was thoroughly depressing. The poor minibus still lay sadly on its side, a reminder of their planned jaunt that had come so suddenly to an end. Everyone brightened, however, when the same two policemen stamped their way out of the mud and into the hostel.

"The diggers will be here soon. You might be able to leave this evening but be warned the roads are still treacherous in places. I would strongly advise you to stay another night and leave in the morning. The forecast is better for tomorrow."

"We only just got out ourselves this morning," said the second policeman. "We can get some food supplies to you if you give us a list of what you need urgently."

"Have you been stuck between the landslides all this time, like us?" queried Helen.

"Yes. Jim here lives further down the way, so we have been operating from his house."

"I have a patient who needs to get to a hospital," said Gloria. "Is that possible?"

"Can she walk a bit?"

"Yes. She has a broken arm."

"If you can get ready to leave while Jackson tells me what he needs, we'll take her now."

"I'll come with her," said Gloria.

There was a scramble to pack up Vera's and Gloria's bags, and with hugs and kisses, they were waved off. The four stumbled through the rocks and mud, holding on to each other until they reached the police car some distance away, parked on the clean roadway. Later Gloria and Vera were helped through another rubble-strewn section where the diggers were working. Beyond, they could see the ambulance was waiting, summoned for them by the police radio.

Back at the hostel, talk had turned to sadness and anger for what Vera had had to suffer.

"We all have terrible things to put up with," said Helen. "Sometimes there's nothing else we can do but put up and shut up," she continued bitterly.

"You sound as if you have a story to tell," said Phil.

"Confess Helen. What's been your cross to bear?" said Rene, half-joking.

"My mother," was her curt reply. "She drove my husband away, and she makes my life a misery at home. I have actually considered ways I could kill her without being caught. That's the guilt I live with even though I haven't actually done it."

There was silence until Marion said, "I think you need to tell us more."

Before Helen responded, the lights suddenly went on.

"Hallelujah! The power's back on."

"That's going to make lunch a lot easier," said Rene, "but it's going to be a bit of a surprise."

But no one was thinking about lunch. Helen looked embarrassed, and eventually, she began to expand on what she had already admitted.

"My mother behaved very badly to Peter. She complained about everything he did. She belittled and mocked him not just to me but to his face. Nothing he could do would please her."

Oh, how he tried, thought Helen remembering all the confrontations. He was patient and forgiving for years, and then he couldn't take it any longer.

"That woman should be in a loony bin," he shouted at Helen. They quarrelled as Helen tried to remind him it was her mother's house they were living in.

"And she never lets me forget it," he added bitterly. "She's mean and spiteful, and I don't know how you can't see what she's doing, not just to me and to us, but to you too."

"She's my mother. We can't throw her out of her own house."

"No? Well, I'm sorry lass, I will have to be the one to leave."

He packed a case and left that night.

Helen was devastated, but her mother crowed and poured out a litany of vitriolic deprecations.

"I always told you he was no good."

This was patently not true. Peter was a decent man, an accountant. They met when his firm sent him to audit the accounts of her employers and, she was tasked with looking after him, ensuring he had all the documents he needed. They hit it off straight away and over the next few months were so comfortable in each other's company that marriage followed quite naturally.

He was sharing a flat with his unmarried brother, and it seemed to make sense that when they returned from their honeymoon, he move into Helen's home. He loved the garden and quickly rescued it from the neglect it had suffered since Helen's father died. For her mother, however, it was just another subject for complaint. He made too much noise cutting the hedge, and she didn't like the way he cut it anyway. The grass was cut too short or not often enough. It was too early to plant bulbs. It was too late to prune roses; it went on and on.

Helen looked round her friends and shook her head sadly.

"Of course, we were divorced when Peter met someone else. I never told my mother that. I let her think we were still married. Just last week, she said to me that I was waiting for her to die so that I could bring "that man" back into her home."

"Was she always like that?"

"Yes, she was. She sent my father to an early grave long before his time. When the school advised my father that I showed some musical talent, my father moved his parents' piano to our house for me to practice. She was furious because where he put it replaced her precious display cabinet full of her collection of Doulton ladies and Beswick animals. It ended up on the upstairs landing ousting an old chest of drawers that got squashed into one of the bedrooms. She said it was a dirty old piano, probably full of woodworm, which it wasn't, and now she'd have to listen to me banging away on it. In fact, it was a lovely instrument that had been tuned regularly and lovingly polished. My father remained unmoved by her screams of fury. Later when I started singing, she complained about listening to my caterwauling. She demanded to know who told me I could sing because it gave her headaches.

"What a horrible thing to say!" said Marion.

"My father retired into his books. He was a bit of an armchair mountaineer and explorer. This infuriated her even more. The more bitter she became, the more headaches she suffered. Sometimes, when she goes to her bed with a headache, it's a blessed peace for me. I get tired of her moans. She doesn't like my cooking; she pushes food around her plate and asks what it is supposed to be; you don't put carrots in shepherd pie. Well, I do. You haven't changed my sheets. I changed them yesterday—it never stops. She nags me about my weight, and the more she nags me, the more pounds I put on. I know it's comfort eating. I just can't stop myself. Now, do you see why I have to stifle thoughts of crushing sleeping pills in her coffee and a pillow or plastic bag over her head?'

Helen was out of breath after this outpouring. Her raw emotion was there for all to see. There was silence, but it was suddenly shattered by Mr. Jackson positively bounding into the room declaring, "We're on the News!"

The newscast told of the lady choristers heading for the Eisteddfod, caught between landslides being looked after by the youth hostel. Their relatives had been assured on Saturday morning, that they were all safe and well and the weather forecast was good. Mr. Jackson was enjoying his moment of notoriety. Things were looking up. In fact, the sun was now shining once more.

Since the promised supplies had not yet arrived, Rene served up lunch. Thanks to the return of electricity, the deep fat fryers were pressed into service for the only food ingredient left. Lunch consisted of potato chips.

* * * * *

They heard the mighty machines long before they appeared, great lumbering monsters crawling up the hill, ducking, scooping, shifting the mud and rocks before them. It was slow and very noisy but fascinating to watch. Eventually, late on in the afternoon, the roadway in front of the hostel was cleared as well as the forecourt. One of the gangs pointed to the minibus and pantomimed righting it. Marion went out with the keys to unlock the doors. Ropes were put around and through the vehicle, and it was pulled upright with apparent ease. One of the men got in and tried the engine, which gave a bit of a splutter but then started.

"Good as new."

"Could you drive it over there for me?" asked Marion, pointing to the hostel forecourt.

"Sure," he nodded; once it was appropriately parked, he handed back the keys with a warning.

"The roads are still very sloppy, and some are crumbling at the edges, so be very careful. Take it slowly."

"I think we are waiting till tomorrow to head home," said Marion.

"A good idea. It should be better by then. We heard about you on the telly. Best of luck."

While Marion was talking to the road gang, the police car had pulled in, and boxes were being carried inside. The Jacksons and Rene were happily taking delivery of the much-needed food supplies.

"Are we all agreed that we stay for another night?" asked Marion once they were all together again...... "and if Mr. and Mrs. Jackson will put up with us," she added.

"It's the sensible thing to do," said Helen. "We need a proper meal and by the time we've had that it will be awfully late to set off."

Trust Helen to be thinking of her stomach, thought Phil. Helen had been the one most put out by having to make do with an equal share of the lunchtime chips despite being the one who most needed to diet. Still having heard how Helen, like Vera, had suffered so much anguish, real torture, whether mental or physical, could be forgiven her weakness.

"We'll leave early in the morning," said Marion, "and stop for lunch somewhere. Right now, I'm going to wash the mud off our transport."

"I'll help you," said Evelyn.

Both went off to get buckets of water and cloth.

In a happier mood, they settled down to wait for dinner which, Rene had declared would be a banquet. She and Phil were busy in the kitchen, and Helen had already set plates and cutlery on the tables. She and Katherine stood at the window watching Marion and Evelyn at work.

"They don't look as if they need any help," commented Katherine.

"No, they're managing nicely," agreed Helen, who had no intention of offering any help. She turned back into the room and applied herself to the jigsaw on the card table that someone had started earlier. It was a colourful view from the air of America's Grand Canyon. Marion and Evelyn came bustling out.

"It's lovely out there now the sun is warm. If it weren't for the road being so messy, I would suggest we all went for a walk."

"Grub up," cried Rene. She would very much have liked to tell them that her list of essential supplies would have been somewhat different from Mr. Jackson's, but hey, they had meat and they could eat, wasn't that the Burns Supper Grace?

"It ain't the Ritz but it will do the job. For starters, we're having chicken soup. Sorry, it's packet soup, but I've added some oomph from the spice rack. Then we're having Shepherd's Pie, and for pudding there's Arctic Roll, Biscuits, and Cheese to follow with tea and coffee. Bon appetite."

Later, replete, they listened to Helen and Rene calculating what they needed to pay the Jacksons.

They had kept a careful note of all the food items they had consumed but were aware of other costs, such as the number of logs burned in the stove. Tonight, the stove was dark and empty, but the heat of the sun had seeped in, and they were warm enough without it. The remaining brandy and whisky dispensed to add cheer somehow created a feeling of anti-climax. Phil, who sat opposite Evelyn, suddenly realized that of all their fellow travellers, Evelyn was the only one who had not shared any secrets or confessed any sins. Indeed, they knew very little about her.

"It's your turn now, Evelyn. We have all bared our souls. What are your guilty secrets?'

"You don't want to know," replied Evelyn.

"Yes, we do."

"Truly, you don't. It's horrible. The worst."

"It can't be any worse than we've heard already."

"It is."

"Come on."

"All I will tell you is that Evelyn Sinclair is not my real name. I am Ailsa Forbes. When I married, I became Ailsa

Barossi, and now I am Evelyn Sinclair, which was my grandmother's name."

"You never told us you had been married."

"Why did you change your name?"

"I didn't want to be found. I was hiding. I'm still hiding."

"From what?"

Evelyn realized, too late, that she had said too much to expect her friends to leave it there. What would it be like to tell her story after such a long time?

"I shot my husband with his own gun and then ran away."

There was silence, and then Phil asked, "You killed him?"

"I think so. I don't know because I ran away." Evelyn was already regretting her admission. She was shaking and holding her hands over her face. Helen put her arms around her and said, "I'm sure you're not a killer."

"Of course not," said Rene. "Tell us what happened."

Evelyn slowly sat up straight, tears in her eyes, and started to recount the events that led to her nightmare flight from what she had done.

* * * * *

"So, what do we call you, Ailsa or Evelyn?" asked Rene.

"Please, just Evelyn. I don't ever want to be Ailsa again."

"Well, you must tell us the whole story. Start at the beginning."

Evelyn paused, took a deep breath, and spoke softly.

"It started a long time ago—when I was still at school, in Aberdeen. My mother worked in a really big hotel. It was a lovely hotel that had once been a huge mansion house. They did a lot of functions, weddings, and conferences, and when they needed extra waitresses, I could make some money. Mum also got me a summer job in the hotel, changing the beds and doing the rooms. That's when I met Frank. He was staying there with his father." It was clear from the dreamy expression on Evelyn's face that this part of her story brought happy memories. She continued, "Frank's father was often away somewhere, leaving Frank alone with nothing to do. He was bored. He started following me around and trying to chat me up. When my shift was up, he was waiting to walk me home, which wasn't very far, and then we started taking a longer route home. We went to the cinema and the cafe, we went swimming, and with borrowed bikes, we went cycling."

Evelyn paused again, becoming Ailsa once more, and remembered the picnics and the fun. She was fifteen that year. Frank was twenty, a real grown-up. He bought her lovely gifts, and she was thrilled. Her father was none too happy about their relationship. His opinion, often expressed, was that Frank had too much money and was too self-confident by half. Inevitably, whatever deals Frank's father had been busy with were concluded, and they were returning to America. Ailsa was devastated. Frank had actually invited her to go with them. She was over the moon, but of course, that notion was stamped upon immediately. She had to return to school. They bade each other a fond farewell promising to write. Her dad assumed it would fizzle out but as good as his word, Frank did write, sometimes two or three letters a week and the parcels with gifts frequently came, becoming more and more extravagant. Her father could only watch and fume. She was ecstatic.

Time went by, but nothing stopped the flow of letters or extinguish their attachment. Coinciding with her leaving school when she was seventeen, Frank asked her to marry him via a transatlantic telephone call. Of course, she said yes, and the next mailing brought a solitaire diamond ring for the engagement. Ailsa's father was furious and refused to let her wear it. Even her mother couldn't make him relent.

Things were only going to go one way. Because she had been on a school trip to Scandinavia, she had her passport, and when Frank sent her a one-way ticket on Transworld Airways, she left home with her father's imprecations ringing in her ears.

"Don't ever come crawling back here when your fancy man dumps you." Her mothers were tearful recriminations, "Please don't go. Your father thinks you are so ungrateful. He saved up so you could go to university, and you're throwing that away. He says you've been dazzled by what he calls your slick Yank."

Sitting hemmed in by a large man on one side and a couple on the other as they flew across the Atlantic Ocean, she was a bit scared but confident of future happiness. She unfastened the gold chain around her neck, removed the ring, and put it on her finger. She would soon be joining her fiancé. Both men had long ago fallen asleep, and both were snoring and snorting loudly, but the woman was as wide awake as Ailsa.

"I noticed you putting on your ring," she said to Ailsa, "Have you just got engaged?"

"I've been engaged for quite a while, but now I'm going to Chicago to be married."

"You're very young to be marrying. Are your parents with you?"

"No. They don't approve. I left home."

"You're travelling alone?'

78

Ailsa nodded, too emotional to speak. The enormity of what she was doing very nearly overwhelmed her. There in the semi-dark, the whole story tumbled out. She explained about her bigoted father and her scatty, ineffective mother. Her only brother was much older and distant. As she had been an unexpected late baby, she was always regarded as troublesome. She described how she had found love with Frank.

"My Dear, how romantic!" said the woman. "I do wish you well."

Arriving at O'Hare Airport was daunting. The terminal was huge and frighteningly busy. Ailsa was bewildered by the sights and sounds. As calmly as possible, she collected her suitcase and stood still looking for Frank to appear. An overweight man in a shiny suit approached her.

"Would you be Miss Forbes?" he asked.

"Yes, I'm Miss Forbes."

"Frank sent me to collect you."

All the way over the Atlantic, Ailsa had dreamed of the moment she would rush into Frank's arms. This wasn't how it should be.

"So you're Frank's trophy wife from England?" he said as he picked up her suitcase.

"I'm not Frank's wife yet, and I don't come from England," she said stiffly. "I'm from Scotland."

"Huh. Come on, the car's this way."

Expecting to sit in the front, she was surprised when he opened the rear door, cupped her elbow, and propelled her into her seat. He then slid into the driver's seat.

"My name's Chuck."

Ailsa didn't care what his name was; she was not happy. The drive was terrifying. The traffic seemed impossibly and dangerously fast. It was a big limousine, but that only made her feel very small and more vulnerable. Arriving at imposing white stone posts, the metal gates between them magically opened for them to pass through and closed silently behind them. She was to learn later this was not wizardry but electronic gadgetry. A short tree-lined drive led to an equally imposing colonial-style house also in white stone. Standing in the doorway at the top of wide, shallow steps was Frank. He was wearing a white shirt and smiling broadly. Yes, it was her Frank, but she was shocked to see that, like Chuck, he was seriously overweight. The hug he gave her and the familiar voice were reassuring.

"Welcome, honey. Did you have a good flight?"

She was glad he hugged her again and kissed her, so she didn't have to answer. In fact, she was struck dumb as they entered the house. It was like a movie set.

"You've already met Chuck. Anywhere you want to go, he'll take you." An elderly man approached them.

"This is Thomson. He's the butler. He runs the place. Anything you need, ask him."

"You must be tired," said Frank, and indeed she was exhausted after a long time with no sleep and then the anxieties. All she wanted at that moment was to be in bed alone.

"I couldn't sleep on the plane, and there's so much to take in. Can I leave it all till the morning?" She could hardly believe she was saying that when she had so much looked forward to being with him and seeing her new home.

"Of course, sweetheart. I'll show you to our bedroom." At the word "our," she must have shown her hesitation. He quickly led her up the thickly carpeted staircase and threw open the door of a spacious bedroom.

"This was my parents' room, but now it's mine ours."

He must have seen the look of panic on her face.

"Don't worry. For now, it's yours. I'll sleep in my old room, but not for long. I've got the wedding arrangements on the go. Toni will unpack your bag. Sleep as long as you like." With another hug and a lingering kiss, he left her. Toni turned out to be a woman in an overall who deftly closed the curtains and turned down the bedcover before asking for the key to Ailsa's suitcase. Ailsa was too tired and bewildered to object, even though she would rather have unpacked for herself. On autopilot, she located the luxurious bathroom, washed away the travel grime, and climbed into bed, asleep almost as soon as her head hit the pillow.

* * * * *

Ailsa slept deeply and wakened late. Despite the late hour, Frank was just starting breakfast when she came downstairs.

"Hi, honey! Take a seat," he said without rising himself.

"We don't get home from the Club 'til two or three most nights so we don't get up early. Have whatever you want."

Frank's plate was heaped with pancakes, and he was pouring maple syrup over them from a large jug. He had bacon on the side. Thomson was pouring from a large coffee pot. Ailsa didn't feel very hungry, so she settled for one pancake and coffee.

"Eat up. We're gonna get you some new clothes," he said, looking at her neat pleated skirt and fine wool jumper, "and you need something special for tonight. I'm gonna introduce you to everyone. They'll just love you," he added happily.

Ailsa assumed, when they set off in the car with Chuck driving, that they would go to a dress shop or a department store, but the large plain grey stone building they entered turned out to be a warehouse with rows and rows of all kinds of clothes. She had never had any great interest in fashion, so she was relieved when Frank took over the selection, mostly dresses, some jackets, and lots of underwear and nightclothes. Frank was clearly enjoying himself like a small boy with a new toy. All Ailsa had to do was supply her sizes, hoping she was right about the different measurements in America. Shoes were next before they moved into a further section full of glittering evening gowns and party dresses. Here Frank picked out a dozen dresses and carried them through to the fitting room, and she had to try them on. Frank watched as the woman in charge pinned tucks and marked hemlines for shortening. It was clear Frank liked a lot of leg and deep cleavage on show. Ailsa would have chosen very differently had she been allowed. Skimpy skirts or long ones slashed to the hip and an abundance of sequins were not her style at all, but what could she do? She had burned her boats and must fit into Frank's way of life.

As they were leaving, Frank said," The hairdresser is coming at five." Then he added, "I reckon my mother's furs should fit you. They're in cold storage. I'll get Chuck to go get them."

Later that day, two full-length mink coats, one in black, one honey-coloured, a short fluffy grey jacket, and a white fur-trimmed stole, were delivered to her room. Ailsa's only experience with fur had been her mother's heavy, stiff musquash coat. She hadn't known that fur could be so light and cuddly, so easy to slip on. She guessed they must be mink. She felt like a princess, her feelings of doubt about the other clothes fading.

She went downstairs just as a small man was coming in with Chuck.

"I have to style your hair," he said and led her through to a room that was obviously also a barber's. Two hours later, her hair was piled up in an elaborate style that, to Ailsa, was pure Hollywood. It was even sprinkled with sparkly glints. She wondered how she would get rid of them at bedtime.

She put on the dress Frank had chosen for her first night at the club. Toni was on hand to zip her into it. It was very tight and boned so that she was forced to stand tall with her breasts pushed up and out. She barely recognized herself in the mirror, looking more like twenty-seven than seventeen. Her feelings were mixed. She looked grown-up and glamorous, yet she was embarrassed by the low neckline. Frank, however, was absurdly delighted with her appearance which was reassuring. He was eager to show her off to what he called the "hip crowd."

They were driven first to a restaurant for dinner. Ailsa was aware that Chuck was clearly not just a chauffeur as he called Frank by his first name and sat down for the meal with them. It was bewildering. Something else that confused Ailsa was that no money seemed to have changed hands, not at the warehouse, the hairdresser, or at the restaurant. Frank must have accounts everywhere. The tightness of her dress constrained her appetite, but Frank and Chuck ate voraciously.

Ailsa's initial impression of the club was not good. As soon as they entered, the loud music was ear-shattering, and in the dim lighting, you could see the heavy haze of cigarette smoke and the hint of cigars. She couldn't stop herself from coughing, and her eyes were already beginning to nip and water. There was a small apron stage surrounded by small tables, but they walked on past those into the casino's gaming rooms where the noise was a little less, but the smoke, if anything, was worse. They spent several hours there, talking to the customers. Ailsa didn't like any of the people Frank had her meet and she was soon bored, but if this was Frank's world, and she was going to be his wife, she would have to get used to it.

Most nights followed the same pattern. At five o'clock, the little man arrived to shave Frank and put Ailsa's hair up. Sometimes there was a young woman who brought an extensive make-up kit. Ailsa wondered if her real self was still there behind the immaculate mask and the theatrical clothes. Chuck drove them to the restaurant, and the three dined together and often with others joining them......important people she had met previously: senators, lawyers, police chiefs, film actors, and sometimes characters her father would have called unsavoury. The nights she enjoyed much more when Frank took time off the club and casino and together, they would watch a movie in the little ten-seater cinema in the basement. Frank loved Disney films and comedies but, occasionally there would be a film that shocked her with a level of violence that wouldn't be shown in a public cinema and, she was too shy to comment on the amount of sex in them. She supposed they must be what she had heard described as adult movies.

One evening she overheard Thomson asking Maria, the cook, for sandwiches for ten people as there was to be a film party, but when they arrived, all men, Frank said, "Go to bed, Sweetheart. This is for us guys only." Ailsa didn't think they were there to watch Disney. One morning Frank said, quite casually, "This was my mother's birthday. It was always a special day. That's why I chose it for us. We're getting married tonight."

Ailsa was stunned. Didn't they have to call banns in America? She had no wedding dress. When she pointed that out to him, he shrugged and said it didn't matter what she wore; she would look beautiful anyway. She was appalled. In her collection of gowns, there was only one white one, Greek-style chiffon with pearl decoration on the bodice, but it was low-cut like all the rest. With one of the day dresses there was a little white jacket, waist length with short sleeves. Wearing that with the dress, she felt it more appropriate for this, her big day. Oh, why couldn't Frank have told her earlier so she could have gone to look for a dress herself?

The hairdresser brought a coronet of white flowers, and her hair was left loose and softly styled around it. Toni told her she looked lovely, but she still couldn't help feeling disappointed. Then, to her surprise, Frank and she travelled together, not to the restaurant, but straight to the club. There she was introduced to Pastor Brown, who was to marry them. He was wearing a purple cassock with his dog collar and sporting a large medallion on a chunky chain. Frank and the Pastor led Ailsa onto the stage. All the tables were full, and every eye was on the three of them as they took the traditional vows. This did not take long, and when Pastor Brown pronounced them man and wife, the audience applauded, and the champagne corks began popping at every table. The new Mr. and Mrs. Barossi were toasted.

Ailsa thought there were plenty of witnesses, but there was no register to sign. Maybe they don't do that in America. As it had been more like a theatrical show than a service, she wondered if they were actually married. However, they had made their vows, and that was that. Much, much later, Ailsa learned that Pastor Brown was a defrocked priest with a gambling habit who had been coerced into playing his part in the "wedding".

As soon as they downed a few glasses of champagne, Frank hustled her out to the car, and Chuck drove them home. Ailsa was a little tipsy. She had drunk more than usual but hadn't eaten since breakfast. Frank hurried her upstairs, and as they entered the bedroom, he was already shedding his clothes, but he was surprisingly considerate as he unzipped her dress and carefully pulled it down. She shimmied out of her panties as she was propelled onto the bed.

"I've waited a long time for you," he said, but even in his haste, he was gentle with her, talking her through her first experience of intercourse until the natural passion took over. Despite his bulk, he was surprisingly agile, and when she shut her eyes, he was again the Frank she had fallen in love with in Aberdeen.

* * * * *

I'm just a bird in a gilded cage, thought Ailsa. Not that she was locked up. Frank said Chuck would take her anywhere she liked, but she didn't know where to go. She had no friends. None of the people she met at the club had asked her to visit them. She had explored the house and garden. She enjoyed being in the garden. There was a lot of grass and big flower beds. There were many bushes, and there was a separate herb garden. They didn't have much of a garden in Aberdeen, but her mother was keen on cooking and liked to use fresh herbs, so Ailsa knew all the herb names but had no idea what the flowers or shrubs were. When she spoke to the gardener, he just nodded back. From Frank she learned that he spoke no English and that he was married to Maria, the cook, whose English was poor but adequate. They lived in a small lodge that Frank's father had built for them at the far end close to the sheds and greenhouse.

Ailsa noticed they used the wooden gate beside the sheds, and she thought it odd that anyone could walk in there, while at the front there were those huge locked metal gates. The wooden gate opened onto a street, which led to a road with bus stops, bicycles, and real people. Although she often slipped through the gate and walked around the neighbourhood, she didn't go far for fear of getting lost. It was an extensive area of large residences. No one she saw spoke to her. They just hurried on their way. It was an aimless existence. They had breakfast when other people would be lunching, and Frank spent most of his afternoons at his big desk in what was called the library, although there were very few books in it. She didn't go there since Thomson had said to her, "Mr. Barossi doesn't like to be disturbed when he's in the library." She took the hint.

Although she had briefly known Frank's father when they were at the hotel in Aberdeen, she wished she had known him better. She knew that Thomson, Toni, Maria, and her husband had been employed by the Barossi family for many years, but she didn't think Chuck belonged to that group. Thomson seemed to avoid him.

One morning, Frank announced they were going sailing. This sounded like an exciting treat, and indeed, the boat was a delightful cabin cruiser beautifully clean and polished. The Skipper was old and weather-beaten with a white stubbly beard and periwinkle blue eyes. He wore a well-worn jersey and a bandana knotted at his throat. Ailsa liked him at once. There were others on board, men in city suits looking oddly out of place. They were clearly ill-at-ease and had been arguing loudly. Frank suddenly ordered her below deck. Instead, she slipped into the wheelhouse and watched in horror as one man was knocked down, then beaten and kicked until he was motionless. Ailsa went to run out to him, but the Skipper laid his hand on her arm and said, "You didn't see that. Stay quiet."

The victim's body was dragged across the deck and then rolled overboard. Frank said, "OK guys, back to business."

"You didn't see that either," said the Skipper clasping her hand tightly. "For your own good, be careful and say nothing."

All the time, Ailsa wondered if Frank's activities were entirely legitimate, she could not have conceived he would be a cold-blooded killer, even if he hadn't actually taken part in the lethal beating. Right that moment, she felt very young and wished she was home in Aberdeen with her parents.

Shortly after the incident on the boat, Ailsa spotted two of the men she thought had been on the boat, chatting, apparently amicably, in the casino at the club. She kept silent watch.

Frank was drinking Vodka which was unusual. Usually, he only drank a glass or two of champagne and perhaps a glass of Vodka before they went to bed. She always did her best to be pleasant and sociable to the customers and staff alike but was determined to steer clear of these two.

One night, Frank went off to the club earlier than usual without waiting for her to have her hair and make-up done. Chuck didn't come back for her. They were back earlier than usual, and Frank was very drunk. Chuck manhandled him through the front door and on up the stairs calling over his shoulder that he would put him in bed. When he came down again, Chuck said, "He's asleep already......in his old bedroom."

"What happened?" asked Ailsa.

"Nothing. He just had a bad night. Two or three guys were winning big amounts. Frank thinks it's a syndicate, and they're cheating, but he doesn't know how. He'll get over it. It's not the first time. Ring me if you need me."

Ailsa knew the number of the direct telephone line to Chuck's studio flat above the garage. She had never used it but was reassured by his concern and availability.

In the morning, Frank seemed his usual self. He apologised quite sweetly for getting home drunk and gave no hint of why he had drunk so much. However, Ailsa could see that he was drinking more at home as well as at the club. Should she maybe suggest to him to cut down? She had long thought she ought to be suggesting he cut down on the amount of food he ate because he was getting even fatter. However, she was afraid what his reaction might be if he thought she was criticising or complaining. She remained silent but wary.

How far had things moved from the fairy tale it had been at the start?

* * * * *

On one of the all-male evenings at the house, Ailsa had gone to bed. She was almost asleep when Frank came into the bedroom.

"Come with me," he said. "There's someone who wants to meet you."

She started to protest, but the hard look in his eyes changed her mind. She quickly donned a dressing gown and followed him into another bedroom, where she was appalled to see a naked man sprawled across the bed.

"Come on, honey. We need a bit of variety in our sex life. You and John here, and I can watch."

Ailsa was rooted to the spot as the realization of what Frank was suggesting sunk in.

"No," she said, "no, no, no!" She fled back to her room. Frank stormed in after her.

"That was very rude," he shouted. "I need you to keep John happy."

"No."

"What do you mean 'No'?"

"No, I don't want that. I don't know how you can ask me to."

"What you want doesn't matter, you stupid cow. I promised him a night with you instead of his winnings at the wheel. He won a lot. You should be flattered."

"No. I thought I was special to you," she said tearfully.

"And so you are, babe, especially if I can watch and film and make some money. You see, there's more old men who would like a night with you, and I would have a hold on them if I could accuse them of raping my wife. Come on."

He gripped her arm and tried to pull her towards the door, but she wrenched free of his grip and stumbled into the bathroom and quickly locked the door shouting another emphatic "No."

It was a very long time before she crept out of the bathroom. Everywhere was silent. She became very calm. She would not be staying here any longer. She retrieved the small suitcase she had brought with her from Scotland and packed a few essentials. She took the rings from her fingers and placed them on the dressing table. Then she brushed her hair out into a simple ponytail. Her passport was still in her old shoulder bag but, of course, she would need some money. She knew where Frank kept cash, and a revolver, in the top drawer of his desk. She would just take enough to get her away from the city. On an impulse, she also took the gun. She put on her raincoat and tied a headscarf over her hair.

When Frank saw her, he started cursing.

"Damn you, you scrawny bitch!"

He said some horrible things and threatened violence. She knew all too well what he was capable of, so when he tried to get up from the chair, she levelled the gun at him.

"You're not going to stop me from leaving," she said. He laughed and spat out more obscenities.

"Get back upstairs."

"No."

"Don't you say 'No' to me."

Her resentment welled up until she felt choked with emotion and disgust. His face was flushed, and he was slobbering with anger into the rolls of fat around his jowls. His shirt was open, and his fat belly spilled out over his knees. Suddenly she saw red. She aimed the gun at his groin and fired. The gun, of course, bucked, and the red stain that blossomed was in the middle of his chest. His startled look was almost comic.

* * * * *

Ailsa giggled and instantly became Evelyn again, sobbing hysterically. Her friends, who had been enthralled by her narrative, tried to comfort her.

"Did he die?" asked Rene.

"I don't know. I ran away."

"Evelyn, you were frightened and disgusted. You were barely an adult. Tell us how you got away."

Returning to being Ailsa again, she recounted how she left by the kitchen door unnoticed and slipped through the little wooden gate. She walked quickly to the nearest bus stop, where several people were waiting. Fortunately, she heard one of the passengers asking for the bus station. She did the same. She handed over a note and apologised for not having coins. The conductor didn't even look up as he gave her ticket and change.

At the terminus, she tried to act normally as she scanned the destination on the board but had no idea where she was. Her attention was caught by a family group saying farewells with many hugs and kisses. As they boarded a bus, she followed closely and tried to look as though she was one of them, asking for the same destination. The fare was expensive, so she hoped they were travelling a long way. She sat just behind the family and, at comfort stops, stuck closely to them, so that she wasn't obviously travelling on her own. When they prepared to get off, so did she. They quickly headed off and left her in the centre of what turned out to be a small town in America's Mid-West.

The winking sign of a motel caught her eye, and she booked a room using her grandmother's name. She first cut her hair short and then had a long shower before venturing out to explore where she had landed up. Near the motel was the cafe the motel clerk had recommended. She wasn't hungry, but she knew she must eat and act naturally.

On her way in, she had noticed a sign—kitchen staff wanted. After she had eaten a well-prepared and nicely served meal, she enquired about the job saying truthfully that she had worked in a hotel. They were so short-staffed she was taken on the spot and handed an apron.

Evelyn lived at the motel but spent all her time at the cafe. Sometimes customers left newspapers behind, and she scanned them but never saw any reference to Frank, possibly because they were predominately local newspapers. Nobody asked her where she came from, and she volunteered nothing about herself. She was making good money, and as soon as she thought she had accumulated enough, she intended to head for Canada and thence to Scotland. She would be travelling there as Ailsa Forbes, the name in her passport. If there was a big search for Frank's killer, this might be risky, but she had to try. She was pretty sure that she had never been properly married and that there was no paperwork to link her with Frank, but she couldn't be sure.

"That's all there is," she said sadly. "I've tried to forget it, but I can't. I'm so ashamed. I know Frank was a criminal, so you could say I was a gangsters' moll." She laughed a little shakily.

Helen held Evelyn's hand. "You were caught up in a dreadful situation. You're not a killer even if he did die, and we are all glad you got home to Scotland, aren't we?"

There were nods of agreement. There seemed no more to be said. It was a sombre group that made their way to their bunks and left for home in the morning.

* * * * *

Some months later, Vera could be found supervising the tuning of the Manse piano, an ancient instrument. She had lovingly polished all the woodwork and the brass candle sconces that flanked the music score ledge. The piano tuner revelled in the rich, mellow tone he was coaxing from it. Vera had settled very happily into life in the Manse. Of course, it wasn't a Manse anymore, and Gloria had been delighted to buy the property from the Church of Scotland authorities when it was no longer needed. Her father had been the last incumbent, so on his retirement, the church was decommissioned. Shortly afterwards, both her parents died within a few weeks of each other, and she lived there alone until Vera accepted her invitation to make it her home too.

Gloria and Vera found their tastes so well attuned that, although there was plenty of space to live separately, they enjoyed meals and evenings together. Their companionship, a joy to both. Furthermore, Vera began working at the practice, joining the team of receptionists. She loved it and was growing in confidence every day. Her house was up for sale; all being handled at arm's length by the solicitor. He had hinted that her late husband's business, now in serious financial difficulty, was likely to go into liquidation. Frankly, like Rhett Butler, she didn't give a damn!

Gloria had spoken to her son in Australia. During several calls, she had liked his warm voice and friendly attitude. He was coming soon to meet her. His travel agent had booked a hotel, and he would be in touch as soon as he arrived. Gloria was thrilled and terrified in equal measure. She and Vera had thoroughly cleaned one of the unused bedrooms if she wanted to invite him to stay. Of course, he would probably want to meet his father's family. She was waiting until they were face-to-face before she told him what she knew of them. He had agreed to that.

Marion's life had returned to normal. She tootled around in her little yellow car, played more golf, and enjoyed weekends when Malcolm was at home. She happily joined him at those social and political events when spouses were expected to make an appearance. At school, she avoided the eyes of the senior boys, appearing more aloof than ever. The feelings of self-disgust lingered, but mostly she managed to suppress them by concentrating on the little pleasures, gardening, and walking Paddy. She talked a lot these days to Paddy, her confidante. Paddy wasn't saying anything.

Helen was spent time at the gym, shedding pounds at a satisfactory rate. Her boss had asked her to travel to Hong Kong with him for a month-long trade fair. He was taking his wife too, so Helen knew she would have plenty of time to herself to sight-see, explore and shop.

Gloria helped her find a care home suitable for her mother while she was away. As usual, her mother was kicking up a fuss, but Gloria said she would probably enjoy it once she was there. Indeed. Helen was hoping that if her mother settled, the house could be sold to cover the care home bills. Helen had already invested her own nest egg, which was substantial (her career always paid well) in a snug, stone-built mews cottage with a sunny courtyard furnished with colourful tubs of flowers and herbs. It was currently let out, but she had bought it to move into. Her head was buzzing with interior decoration plans and colour schemes.

Phil and Evelyn resumed their busy lives, both happy to be unnoticed again but liberated by their confessions and truly heartened by the sympathy, acceptance and support of their friends.

Rene, too, was busy, planning and preparing for a buffet supper party to welcome Katherine and Murray home from their extended honeymoon in New Zealand. Everyone was to be invited, including the men of the Kelvin Singers who had not been caught in the Llangollen catastrophe. They had been typically late in leaving for Wales, confident of their ability to eat up the miles speedily. The result was they were turned back by the police, where the major flood was blocking their route. Spouses and partners all would be welcome to this reunion, but only the eight would feel the depth of their strange and special bond.

The End